MUCKLUCK, ALASKA

Where Nothing Ever Happens

By
Lisa Augustine

Published by Aunt Phil's Trunk LLC
6831 Viburnum Drive, Anchorage, AK 99507
www.auntphilstrunk.com

Copyright © 2012 by Lisa Augustine

ISBN 978-0-9849494-1-0
Printed in the United States of America
First Printing July 2012

Cover art by Robert Maske

Note: This book is a work of fiction. Any similarity to persons living or dead is purely coincidental.

FOR TOM

AND

OUR FAMILY

Stacy, Michelle, JT,

Isabella and Sam

With my love and gratitude,

I thank God you are mine!

Author Lisa Augustine sits in her California home surrounded by hats she knits for children who come through crisis centers.

ABOUT THE

AUTHOR

Lisa Augustine was born in 1939 in Seward, Alaska. She grew up in Hope and Kenai, villages located on the Kenai Peninsula, southcentral Alaska. Her family mined for gold on Resurrection Creek near Hope, and during the 1940s and '50s, her mother was postmaster in Kenai.

During those pre-statehood days, and before oil was discovered at the Swanson River near Kenai, Lisa experienced the joys and sorrows of small-town, rustic Alaska.

Although Muckluck is pure fiction, Muckluckers and their stories could have been real. They are typical of Alaskans and their experiences during that era, and Lisa writes of them with great fondness and pride.

Lisa lives with her husband, Tom, in Lincoln, California. They have two daughters, a son-in-law and two grandchildren. She is the author of two books: a historical memoire titled *The Dragline Kid* and a book of poetry, *Cheer Up it could be Verse*.

When not writing, she can be found curled up in her favorite chair knitting hats for children who pass through crisis centers. To date, she has created more than 2,700 caps.

Appreciations

I first and foremost thank my husband, Tom Augustine, for encouraging me to keep writing, for helping me dredge up a word when senior moments struck, for fighting my dragon computer and for keeping me sane throughout the writing process. He deserves a halo, and he has my eternal love.

Laurel Bill, my adopted Alaskan cousin, came to my rescue when I despaired of ever getting Muckluck published. She is the author of the popular *Aunt Phil's Trunk* Alaska history series. Her technical skills, self-publishing experience and distributing know-how continue to amaze me. Without her suggestions, help and generosity, I'd still be knee-deep in exclamation points and dashes, lost in a morass of pre-publishing terror. I can never thank her enough.

Robert Maske, using a photograph of my late mother as a model, turned Kate into a cover girl. He captured my vision of Muckluck and made it a reality in his beautiful cover artwork. I thank Bob for his talent and his patience.

Publisher Jackie Pels of Hardscratch Press, author, editor, my girlhood friend and publisher of my first book, *The Dragline Kid*, supplied me with Russian words I had no idea how to spell. I love you, Chick. Gospodi pomilui!

Rita Kranig read the manuscript and declared it worthy. A self-professed "non-reader," her comments and praise were especially gratifying and encouraging.

And, finally, I thank the courageous, resourceful , wonderful people I grew up with on the Kenai Peninsula back before statehood and the oil companies arrived. Most of the old-timers have gone to their rewards, but I will never forget them, the stories they told and the example they set. They weren't Muckluckers — but they tried to "do the right thing."

MUCKLUCK, ALASKA

Where Nothing Ever Happens

Introduction

Well, I'm an old lady now. It's hard to believe, but there's no getting around it. I don't feel old, though. Oh, I have my aches and pains, but I still think I'm young. Until I look in the mirror and wonder, 'who's that old lady staring at me? What happened? And how did it happen so fast?' Just one of God's little surprises. He sure has a sense of humor!

There were ninety-five candles on my cake at my last birthday party. It's a good thing it was a big cake. When I tried to blow out all those little candles, a pile of paper napkins caught fire. Caused a heck of a fuss among my flock of children, grandchildren, great-grandchildren and one tiny great-great. Lucky for us, one of my gang is a firefighter. He grabbed the fire extinguisher I keep handy just in case and doused the blaze. Completely ruined that pretty cake, but Susanne had brought plenty of assorted cupcakes, which satisfied everyone's sweet tooth, including my own six remaining choppers. I do love sweets, don't you?

I'll admit it. These days I don't always remember who currently lives in the White House, or my own telephone number. But, by gum, I remember a whole lot about what happened when I was in my prime — those precious years when I was between thirty and fifty. Those were the years when I was old enough to appreciate life, and my lifestyle, and still young enough to actually enjoy them.

Those years are so clear in my mind that sometimes, when I'm dozing in my La-Z-Boy, I actually think I'm back in Alaska again. Oh, yes indeed, I remember everything about Muckluck and those dear souls who proudly called it home during those wonderful, bygone days. If you have the time, maybe you'd like to hear a story or two. You would? Good! You caught me in the mood to reminisce.

Pull up a chair. Take a load off. Would you like a cuppa coffee? No? Well, how about some sweet tea, then. There are the fixin's on the counter — help yourself. I still prefer my coffee strong and black as tar, and I don't care if it's a day or two old, either. If I doze off while I'm talking, just give me a poke and I'll finish the story.

I should tell you right off the bat that I was born in Muckluck in 1912 and lived there until I was in my sixties. Never had any desire to live any place else. But when my husband died, my kids insisted I move Outside to be closer to them. So here I am in Tacoma. My kids were worried about me "way up there in Alaska." As if I couldn't take care of myself. Pshaw! Oh well, that's the way it goes — the child becomes the parent and the parent becomes the child. If you live long enough, that's what happens. And there ain't a darn thing you can do about it.

But I wasn't always old. Once I was as full of beans as you. Some folks might say I was full of piss and vinegar, but that's going a little too far, don't ya think? I try to keep a civil tongue in my head.

My ma raised three young ones under "extreme" conditions, but we all managed to turn out pretty good. She was a hard worker and a strict taskmaster, but she was fair and loving. Daddy was a gold miner, a trapper, a logger, and sometimes he worked on the road crew. Anything to make an honest dollar. But the real passion of his life was mining; even when he held other jobs, he always found time to do some panning — always searching for that elusive gold. He worked way too hard, and he died suddenly, way too young.

Ma struggled to keep us going, and when she passed, my brother and sister went Outside to get an education. They never came back to Alaska. I took over the home place and stayed there, struggling just like Ma. It was my choice, and I was satisfied with my lot.

I was happy to read whatever I could get my hands on as a child, including cereal boxes and hunting regulations. I'd sit for hours, drawing pictures or writing short stories and poetry. My family thought they were pretty good, too. I've kept some of them over the years, and I suppose I had some talent.

Because Muckluck was such a small village, I didn't have many friends. But those I had were top drawer. In the long days of summer, we spent hours on end playing hide-and-seek, kick-the-can and hopscotch. And we loved exploring the woods, building forts and helping to stock our families' cupboards and root cellars with edibles from nature, like berries, mushrooms, fiddlehead ferns.

During the dark days of winter, we played board games, read, played in the snow, skated on the lake and held fierce snow-ball battles. We were never bored because we used our active imaginations. Not like kids today who have to be "entertained" every minute. Lordy, don't get me started on that.

But you don't need to hear about my family. I want to introduce you to other folks I knew and loved. This is about Muckluckers who, though most have gone to their rewards, are as alive to me today as they were all those years ago.

I recall a young fella who'd just graduated from high school back then. He declared loud and clear, "I can't wait to get out of this place. Nothing ever happens in Muckluck."

Well, I aim to prove him wrong. You tell me what you think.

My Father's Mistress

Alaska whispered in his ear:
"Come to me, I've riches here.
I will share them all with you.
Hidden, secretly I wear them;
From my bosom you must tear them.
I will make your dreams come true."

"Come to me, I'm waiting for you.
Come and know me, I implore you.
Bring your strength and youth to me.
Come and taste my untold treasure,
Golden riches without measure.
Come and love me, come and see."

Thus Alaska sought and claimed him.
And a "Sourdough" they named him.
Thus he sold his youth for naught.
Searching, searching, never finding,
Still her promises were binding
Tempting with the gold he sought.

When at last his health had faded
And his dreams became too jaded,
Gold he knew would never be his prize.
Still he loved Alaska's glory;
She became his life-long story.
He began at last to sadly realize:

She would test you, she would take you,
She would bend you and would break you
As she beckons with her tantalizing song.
She would steal your dreams and haunt them
Till you swear that you don't want them,
Then she'd laugh and prove to you that you'd been wrong.

But oh, dear friend, the glory
As you undertake the story
That unfolds, and face the challenge of each day.
You will know when journey's ended
Though you've broken, or you've bended,
That you've lived a life somewhere along the way!

~ 1 ~

The door slammed against my back as I stumbled, panting into my cabin. It nearly knocked me on my face. Late March in Muckluck often brought a mishmash of weather. Some years we had an early "breakup," other winters the snow kept falling well into April. That night a blizzard roared and howled. As I struggled to close the door, the wind flung snow across my worn linoleum floor, making small drifts as it piled against the sparse furniture.

I wrestled the door shut and crunched across the slippery floor, feeling my way in the dark toward the table where the kerosene lamp stood. In the process, I barked my shin on the Victorian footstool Grandma left me. Dad gum, another bruise on my leg.

Yanking snow-crusted mittens off with my teeth, I fumbled for the box of wooden matches. I pulled a stick out, struck it on the side of the box and lit the lamp. The stink of sulfur and kerosene filled my nose, but suddenly the cabin felt warmer — a false impression if ever there was one.

The black, pot-bellied iron stove was out, and at 10-below zero, no lamp could provide any heat to speak of. But it made a comforting glow, casting shadows around the cabin while leaving the corners dark and mysterious.

I dreaded facing the storm again, but my bladder was yelping for relief. In Muckluck, nature's call was answered in nature.

Every household, including those of bachelor sourdoughs, had outhouses with varying degrees of comfort and style. Some were fancy, with corrugated tin roofs and cutout quarter moons in their doors; some had only gunnysack doors; and some, a necessity for large families, were known as "two-holers," for obvious reasons.

My humble outhouse, like my cabin, was old, weathered and drafty. It smelled exactly like you'd expect it to smell. Nasty.

Located about 30 feet behind the cabin, it was sheltered by spruce and willows and was cold as a witch's tailbone that time of year.

I grabbed the lamp and fought my way outside around the cabin. The storm paused occasionally, allowing the moon to peek out for a brief glance before ducking behind snow-laden clouds. I struggled to keep the lamp lit, sheltering it cautiously while trying to keep my wool coat from catching on fire as I waded through drifts nearly to the tops of my boots.

As I approached the toilet, I noticed the door stood partly open. Good — that meant I wouldn't have to battle the snow to get inside. Still, it wasn't easy handling the lamp and pulling the door at the same time. With a final yank, it opened enough so I could peer inside.

And there he sat. His pants down around his feet, gray long johns hiding his privates and legs modestly. His eyes were closed, the lashes and eyebrows white, thick with frost. His black stocking cap, also frosted, covered his hair and slid down his brow. Fur-lined mittens lay on the bench beside him atop a Sears Roebuck catalog. With store-bought toilet paper in short supply, catalogs made a reasonable substitute. And they were something to browse through while you "did your duty."

The man's pale face was slightly blue-tinged, his beard a brown and white tangle. Traces of tobacco juice showed through the rime. He looked peaceful, his chapped, blue lips almost smiling. He was as stiff as the board he sat on, and as dead as it's possible to be.

I won't kid you. I'm no hero. But I'm not usually a complete coward, either. However, the second I realized there was a corpse in my outhouse, I yelped, dropped the lamp, which promptly went out, and backtracked so fast that I plopped on my butt in the snow. After scrambling to my feet, I turned and ran blindly through the whipping, falling snow toward Marshal Olav Thorson's place.

Olav was our marshal by default. No one else in Muckluck wanted the job. The pay was laughable, and anything approaching crime rarely happened in Muckluck.

Olav had been a Scandinavian fisherman who'd fished Cook Inlet enough years to realize he wasn't cut out for the job. He was prone to seasickness and couldn't stand the smell of fish, so he decided to beach his craft. He wandered on over to Muckluck and settled in.

That was around 1935. And thirteen years later, Olav was still there, keeping order in a town too decent to require his services. Still, the U.S. Government, in its "infantile wisdom," decided the miners, sourdoughs, a few wives and children and a handful of Natives needed protection from each other. Olav was it.

I fell against his door, banging weakly with my fist. It was only 9:30 p.m., so Olav was still up — probably playing Solitaire. His shortwave radio was blaring country-western music, so it took a while for him to hear my feeble thumping. Finally, he yanked open the door.

"What's up, Katie?" he asked as he pulled me into the warmth of his small log home.

Panting and gulping air, I flopped into his recently abandoned chair, trying to get my breath as I swiped my sleeve under my dripping nose and gathered my wits. I hadn't even felt the cold, the wind or the snow as I plowed across town to Olav's door. But now that I was inside, blobs of snow dropped from my clothes onto his worn, wooden floor.

Olav waited patiently. His usually calm eyes were filled with concern, and his tall frame bent at the waist as he peered into my face. He was a fine figure of a man, in his forties, and still had most of his straight, dishwater-blonde hair. He'd never married, as far as anybody in Muckluck knew, and he didn't seem to miss having a wife and family. He was comfortable in his own skin and enjoyed his own company. He was a lot like me in that respect, so we could be good friends without complications.

"Olav," I finally gasped, "there's a dead fella in my outhouse! What are you going to do about it?"

"Well," Olav said, as he pondered what I had just told him. He pursed his lips and looked at the ceiling for inspiration.

"I suppose I'd best go take a look at 'im. Do you know who he is?"

"Nope, I didn't recognize him. I don't think he's from around here, but I didn't take a very close look," I said. "I just want you to get him out of my outhouse. I've gotta go — bad."

"Go on out back and use my biffy while I pull on some warm duds. We'll go take a look at this dead fella. I suppose we could call him a squatter," Olav said with a grin.

Olav actually made one of his rare jokes. While I was not in a joking mood, I appreciated the effort. And his offer. I gratefully made my way out back.

~ 2 ~

As we hustled over to my place, the blizzard took a breather. It was a relief not to have to fight our way through the storm, and it was helpful to have Olav's strong hand grasping my elbow as we plowed through the drifts. His powerful flashlight barely showed my stumbling footprints in the snow, leading us straight to my outhouse.

Sure enough, the corpse was still there. He looked exactly as he had a half hour ago — except maybe a little stiffer and a little whiter. Olav poked him in the chest with a sturdy finger. The only response was a soft fart beneath the body. I noted Olav's sly grin. Why do men think passing gas is so darned funny?

"Yup, he's dead all right. Here, you hold the flashlight while I try to get a better look at 'im," Olav said.

I did as I was told, but I didn't much like the assignment.

"Just get him out of there," I begged. "Can you lift him, or should I get Benny to help?"

Benny Carson was my closest neighbor. His place was about 75 yards from where we stood.

"I think I can manage, but it would help if you lent a hand," Olav muttered.

Olav reached under the man's armpits, and with a mighty grunt, tried to lift him.

"Why, he's frozen to the seat!" Olav said. "Now what do we do?"

The marshal contemplated the problem for a minute or two, and then came up with an idea.

"If we had some hot water, we could thaw him out a little," he said. "You go start a fire, fill the teakettle with water and we'll give 'er a try."

I was not at all keen about the idea, but what else could we do?

The temperature was steadily dropping as night fell, so we had to move fast.

About a half hour later, I was back at my privy grasping a boiling teakettle with a pot holder.

"Holy mackerel," Olav said. "We don't want to cook 'im! Put some snow in there and cool 'er down a bit."

Again, I did as I was told.

Soon Olav was carefully pouring warm water around the dead man's posterior. Before long, he was able to pry the body off the toilet bench and we wrestled him out onto the snow. The poor guy was frozen in a seated position, with the trap door of his long johns flapping open in back.

"Don't look, Katie! Go get a blanket, and we'll cover 'im up for the time being." Olav was nothing if not chivalrous — and also a little prudish.

Now I was even more annoyed.

My outhouse, my teakettle, and now my blanket. I am, by nature, not a selfish person. And I was sympathetic to the man who'd cashed in his chips on my property. But I was beginning to feel a bit miffed at the inconvenience he was causing. I was a thirty-six-year-old single woman who liked her privacy and her space, which currently was being crowded by a dead stranger. But I went to get a blanket, as I grumbled under my breath.

More Muckluckers arrived in short order. They'd seen the beam of our flashlight and began to wonder why it was taking me so long at the outhouse. Muckluckers watched out for each other, and our habits were so predictable that anything out of the ordinary drew immediate attention and concern.

After a lot of consideration, suggestions and just plain conversation, Molly Parkins, our postmaster, went and got her sled. We loaded the corpse onto the sled, on his back with his legs in the air at a 45-degree angle, and tied him securely with a rope supplied by Gus Mortenson. A couple of the fellas then took the sled's pull rope, and our little procession headed over to the church of St. Anastasia, where we woke Father Sorinoff.

Father pulled a brown bathrobe over whatever priests wear to bed and took in the situation. He then offered a prayer in Russian and blessed the body, concluding with two words I understood: "Gospodi Pomilui," which means, "Lord have mercy."

He graciously allowed us to use the church woodshed as a temporary morgue. We figured we'd deal with the situation the next morning in daylight. Olav and I were relieved of our burden, and we waded off to our respective cabins for a well-earned night's sleep. The rest of the crowd wandered home, too.

Olav's responsibilities were far from over, however. The next morning he radioed the authorities in Anchorage.

They promised to send an officer as soon as possible. The only way they could do that was by helicopter, since we had no airfield at the time, and the road to Anchorage hadn't been built yet. A man named Brady had recently brought the first helicopter to Alaska, so we lucked out on that score.

We cleared a landing pad in the middle of the schoolyard. In due time, a uniformed policeman and a mousey little guy, who was introduced as the coroner, were examining our frozen visitor. A check of his pockets produced a soiled bandana, a can of Copenhagen, a jackknife and a bottle opener — but not a shred of identification.

The officer asked a lot of foolish questions, made a few notes on a lined tablet and managed to look just a tad interested. Then he yawned and assured us he'd look into the matter. In the meantime, until he could identify the body and inform the next of kin, he suggested we leave the fellow where he was.

The temperature still hovered around 10 degrees below zero, so there was no fear of him thawing out.

Father Sorinoff agreed to host the deceased. He had enough wood stacked in his back porch to last for a while, so our visitor could rest in the woodshed undisturbed.

Now you'd think we'd hear from the authorities in Anchorage PDQ, wouldn't you? We waited several days. Then a week passed. Then two weeks.

Olav's patience finally gave out. He radioed the police to see how the case was coming along. Apparently it wasn't. Anchorage couldn't find any information on our man — or anyone who might know or miss him.

Anchorage didn't want him. So the stranger became our problem.

That's the way it was in those days. You found him, you got him, you keep him. He became, as they say now, "a cold case." No pun intended.

Since there was no sign of foul play, the coroner declared it death by heart failure with subsequent freezing. So the citizens of Muckluck set about to do the right thing.

~ 3 ~

I suppose I should explain about Muckluck before going any further. Back around the turn of the Twentieth Century, gold was discovered on the Kenai Peninsula. A rush of frantic miners followed, and many of them prospected around Resurrection Creek and its tributaries. Towns like Sunrise and Hope sprang up practically overnight.

Two Native brothers, Abe and Gabe Gilbert, staked a claim along a small creek called Moose Run. Soon they found a pocket of high-grade gold. Before long, the area was swarming with men wielding picks and shovels and swirling gold pans as they searched for more rich ore.

Those with more ambition built sluice boxes with riffles and ran pipelines down the mountainside to bring water for sluicing. Some had enough luck to keep hope alive, and they stayed. Those who didn't, moved on to other diggins.

A store and a bar provided the necessities. And soon a little settlement graced the banks of Moose Run.

One day, Abe and Gabe got into a fight over a mukluk. It seems their mother had made them each a pair of the sealskin beauties, and now one of those beaded boots was missing.

I'm told it was Abe who accused Gabe of taking his mukluk. The fight gathered steam, until Gabe finally bashed Abe over the head with an iron skillet, killing him on the spot.

Gabe was hauled off by dog team to the hoosegow in Seward, and the place finally got a name — Mukluk. Before long, someone grumbled that mucking around in Moose Run wasn't bringing much luck. The village wit declared the town should be christened Muckluck, and the name stuck.

It didn't take long before the gold ran out. And so did most of the town's population. But a few stayed on, and ever so often, another seeking soul would find his way to town, move into one of the abandoned cabins, and live off the land, so to speak. Today they call it "subsistence living."

As years passed, some of the men found wives. And as usually happens, before you knew it, there were a couple dozen kids running around Muckluck, making mischief, wading and fishing in the tumbling waters of Moose Run.

Folks sent out a request for a schoolteacher. Soon Thelma Ward arrived with several boxes of textbooks and a chalkboard. We also applied for a post office, and Jeb Parkins was appointed postmaster. When he passed away, his daughter, Molly, took over the job. After all, the general delivery boxes were already set up in the Parkins' cabin, so it seemed reasonable, and the government didn't object. Alaska, being just a territory and not a bona fide state, wasn't given much attention in those days.

So that's how we became a legitimate town — back around 1935. We had all the necessities, including a church, a school, a post office, a general store and some 147 intrepid individuals, give or take one or two. A few dogs hung around, too, as well as a coyote that was staked and penned behind the store.

I'll not guild the lily. Winters in Muckluck were long and cold and dark. But the summers were glorious.

Gardens flourished in fertile soil during the long, sunlit days. Vegetables like carrots, potatoes, cabbage, lettuce, turnips and radishes grew to gargantuan size. Wild berries covered the mountainsides, ready to be picked and preserved as jams or made into cobblers and pies. Every family had enough moose meat, duck, rabbit and fish to keep their stomachs full. The meat, when not eaten fresh, was either canned, salted, smoked or naturally frozen in ice hauled from glaciers and packed in root cellars.

A few of the men still mined. Others worked for the Alaska Road Commission. Two were big game guides, and one family ran a successful lumber mill.

The women were mostly homemakers, but some, with an artsy-craftsy bent, made trinkets to sell in the shops in Seward and Anchorage. Besides the school teacher and postmaster, or postmistress, if you must, there were a couple darn good artists. And for a short while, we had a fella who wrote songs for some of the big-time country singers Outside. Outside being the lower 48 states — or any place else that wasn't Alaska.

We also had a woodcarver, Dave Moffid, who whittled little totem poles, moose and other Alaska critters for the tourist trade. We had our fair share of characters, too, and a couple of certifiable dingbats.

Once a month, weather and roads permitting, a Methodist preacher came over from Seward to hold services at the schoolhouse, and of course, we had the venerable Russian church of St. Anastasia. Actually, it was more of a chapel — quite small, but its blue, onion-shape roof was our pride and joy. How and why Father Sorinoff was sent to Muckluck will forever be a mystery.

Nobody else spoke Russian, but Father said Mass every day, and occasionally a worshipper would join him. St. Anastasia was worth a visit, if only to marvel at the beautiful treasures inside. Its wonders included icons, crosses and thuribles that Father somehow had acquired. We didn't ask, but I'm sure everything was proper, as Father S was an honorable, God-fearing gentleman.

If you're wondering why we didn't know more about Father Sorinoff, it's because we didn't know much about anybody's life before they came to Muckluck. If they didn't feel like telling, we didn't feel like asking. We had the policy of "don't ask, don't tell" long before the U.S. Army did.

For a half century, people came to Muckluck for reasons of their own. Some came to escape families, some to escape the law, some were sick and tired of the rat-race, and some came just to see if they could survive without modern conveniences.

Many found that they couldn't hack it, and after the first winter, they were outta there.

"And good riddance," we said. But those who stayed were a sturdy bunch with big hearts and pure souls. At least that's what we believed. And were darned proud of it, too.

So when we found ourselves in possession of an unidentified and unclaimed corpse, a few of us got together for coffee and fruitcake over at Bev and Smokey Middleton's place and decided to do the right thing. We'd throw the man a funeral and bury him as Muckluck's adopted son.

~ 4 ~

Because of the iffy weather in our neck of the woods, we feared we might experience one of our early spring thaws. That would make digging the grave easier, but it also would make dealing with the body less desirable.

Dave Moffid offered to build the coffin, and Carol Krugger, who had been a nurse in Seattle, said she would "neaten up" the fella a little. I said I'd help her. The Raben twins, Earl and Mack, volunteered to dig the grave. We set to work quickly, since the weather report that night said we were in for some fast warming.

Carol and I didn't do much with the body, except to wash his face and hands and wrap him up in a clean sheet donated by Bing Sultz over at the store. We left his face uncovered but got most of the rest of him wound tight. Then we sat him in an old chair.

Since he was still frozen in a seated position, wrapping him up wasn't the only challenge. But Dave, who was smart enough to not build a rectangular coffin, created a snug, square box into which we lowered our visitor, chair and all. He looked quite regal sitting there, smiling softly, as Dave nailed the lid on tight.

Earl and Mack had to use smudge pots to render the ground soft enough to dig. They were able to make the hole about 10 feet deep, which we felt was respectable. We then lowered our charge into the ground and filled the hole.

Due to the necessity of haste, we held the funeral after the burial. Dressed in his black cassock, Father Sorinoff carried a gold cross and swung a fragrant censor as he chanted Russian prayers. We Muckluckers stood reverently with bowed heads and folded hands.

Thelma had brought an African violet, one of several potted plants from the schoolhouse windowsill. She placed it on the mound of dirt and melting snow.

Kenny Waldorf played his harmonica, while we sang "Amazing Grace," "Heaven is My Home," and finished off with "For He's a Jolly Good Fellow."

There were few dry eyes as Dave pounded a freshly carved wooden plank at the head of the grave. On it were the words:

R.I.P.
WE DO NOT KNOW HIS NAME
NOW HE'S A MUCKLUCKER
ALL THE SAME
March 1948

And that was that. We went back to our individual pursuits, musing on the fast-arriving spring and summer seasons. Our surprise visitor was gone — but not forgotten. For many years, his grave was kept up real nice. Forget-me-not seeds were sprinkled over it each spring, and by summer, the grave was abloom with Alaska's beautiful, but humble, blue state flower.

Who is my brother?
Am I my brother's keeper?
Yes — and he is mine

~ 5 ~

Just as predicted, we had an early breakup that year. By mid-April, the snow had melted and the roads and paths were a quagmire. Folks who'd sent away for seed catalogues started planning gardens — but the ground was too muddy to work. It was an awkward time. Muckluckers craved to get busy, to rouse from their lengthy winter hibernation and set to work on outdoor projects too long postponed.

My cabin needed fresh moss stuffing in the chinking between the logs. The outhouse needed work, too. I asked Dave Moffid to build me a new biffy bench, with maybe a few carved details for fun. I was anxious to get rid of the old bench, as I found it spooky to use after my experience with the recently deceased. I also   wanted to get in some fishing — my new canner needed breaking in.

Minnie Carrington was more anxious than most for spring to arrive. She was expecting their first child around the first of May. Notice that we used to call her condition "expecting" or "with child." Nowadays, to my disgust, they call it a "baby bump" or "preggers." Imagine that!

Minnie and Felix had been married twelve years, and they had just about given up hope of ever producing an heir. They were both in their early forties, so time was running out. Minnie tried every suggestion for conception that came her way. She consumed gallons of beet juice, took Lydia Pinkham's little pills and kept a calendar of her fertile times. She also did a lot of heavy praying. When she finally hit the jackpot, nobody, including Minnie and Felix, knew what actually did the trick. But God had seen fit to send them a child at last.

Felix worked at the Martin sawmill. He came home every evening covered with sawdust, but he smelled deliciously of newly sawed lumber.

Minnie brushed him vigorously from head to toe with her whiskbroom, and then made him take a spit-bath before she'd let him in her bed. Maybe that's why procreation was so long in coming. Such matters are far beyond my understanding.

Be that as it may, the whole town eagerly awaited its new citizen. A bunch of the ladies threw a baby shower, and you wouldn't believe the wonderful gifts they brought. Most of the tiny garments were handmade, sewn on pedal Singer sewing machines, or lovingly knitted or crocheted.

Some of the gals prevailed upon their husbands to contribute, too. Minnie got a beautiful wood cradle from the Waldorf family, a carved bear with wheels and a pull rope from the Moffids, and Bing Sultz's wife, Val, brought a set of tiny silverware from Sultz General Mercantile. One old-timer offered a frozen weasel, but after he departed, so did the weasel.

Minnie planned to get to Seward in plenty of time to have the baby delivered at the small hospital. She'd made arrangements with Izzy Fitzheimer who, once a week, drove his maroon International pickup to Seward over the dirt and gravel road to bring mail and supplies to Muckluck. Once in Seward, Minnie would stay with friends until the baby was ready to make an appearance. But babies arrive when they are good and ready, and this one already had a mind of its own.

In the middle of the night on April 21, Carol came banging on my door. Carol, having been a nurse in her younger days, was usually pretty unflappable. But she was in a dither that night. Panting, and dropping mud off her rubber boots onto my clean lino, she was the picture of flappability.

"Hurry up and come with me!" she ordered.

"What's the matter? Somebody hurt?" I asked, as I pulled my jeans and sweatshirt over my p.j.'s.

"Minnie's fixing to have that baby *now*. Her water broke about half an hour ago, and Felix came for me to assist. Oh Lordy, I worked on the geriatric ward in Seattle, and never even saw a baby born. I need help!"

We set off at double time toward the Carrington's place. The moon, round and white, lit the path. The stars looked near enough to grab hold of. But we didn't hesitate to admire the brilliant night sky. We hustled as fast as the mud sucking at our boots would allow.

When we arrived, we found Felix shuffling back and forth, wearing a trench in the planks of their front porch. He had thrown on a pair of torn jeans and a pajama top, and his hair was sticking up in all directions.

"Esther's in there with Minnie. Thank God you're here," he said. "Minnie's having a hard time. She needs all the help she can get." He tugged at his hair and continued to pace.

Esther Waldorf was Athabascan Indian, the mother of Kenny and his five siblings. There was no doubt in our minds that Esther knew more about birthing babies than Carol and I put together. We were mighty relieved to find her bustling about, heating water on the stove and calmly attending to Minnie, who was lying across the bed on an oilcloth tablecloth covered with a fresh sheet.

Minnie was alternately sobbing and panting, sweating and groaning. We heard Felix, out on the porch, echoing her distress.

Carol and I stood around unhelpfully, watching Esther tend to her patient. Occasionally she'd take a peek, insert a finger, and shake her head. Not yet. After several miserable hours, Esther checked again.

"That baby is gonna come NOW," she said.

Carol and I each grabbed one of Minnie's bent knees. We held on for dear life, while Minnie yowled and Esther positioned herself to catch the baby. Suddenly Esther looked worried. The baby's head had arrived, but a blue umbilical chord was wrapped snuggly around the infant's fragile neck.

Esther knew what to do. She freed that chord, pulling it over the tiny head, and out popped the nastiest-looking little bundle of joy you ever saw. A daughter for the Carringtons.

Esther grasped the child by the heels and gave her a whack on the fanny. The little girl let out a yelp and started to breathe.

Carol took the baby and washed her in the dishpan, while Esther tidied up the new mother. By the time I changed the sheet and set it to soak, the baby was clean and dry and looked almost human.

I forgot to mention that during the long labor, Esther told us an ancient Native custom, guaranteed to bring good luck. She said a newborn child was to be named after the first thing the mother saw when she opened her eyes after that last, long, hard push that brought forth the baby. Native babies were often born outdoors, where the first thing their mothers saw was something from nature like a fern, a jay, a willow bough.

Unfortunately, the first thing Minnie saw was a tin can that sat beside Felix's favorite chair. It once held tomatoes but now was his spit can. Those who chewed "smokeless tobacco" always kept a spit can handy in the house. And while "dipping" was a nasty, smelly habit, it was common among Muckluck men.

Well, you can't name a little girl Spit Can now, can you? But just to be on the safe side, Minnie named her baby Candice. Close enough, and it seemed to work. That was one lucky, much-loved little girl. She grew into a beautiful young woman, who became a teacher, married well and had two terrific children. It seemed to me that she lived a charmed life, maybe due to her name.

Esther only smiled sagely when the subject came up.

The Baby

God sent a precious bundle.
They loved her from the start.
She captivated Mama
And stole her daddy's heart.

And then one day they turned around
And in their baby's place
There stood a laughing girl-child
With bright and shining face.

The years sped all too quickly.
Their little girl had grown
Into a college coed
And their little bird had flown.

One day a handsome stranger
Strode into Daughter's life.
He asked them for their darling's hand
And took her for his wife.

As time went on, they prospered
And their love grew strong and true.
They made a home together
And they made a family, too.

Now she's Mother, Wife and Teacher.
A woman of so many parts.
But she'll always be their baby
At the center of their hearts.

~ 6 ~

Helping deliver a baby wasn't the only medical emergency Carol had to deal with over the years. She always was willing to help out when needed.

Once one of the boys at Martin's sawmill managed to lose the tip of his pointy finger to a saw. Carol stitched him up, gave him a shot of penicillin in the hind end, and he survived. He kept the fingertip in a jar to freak out the girls.

When little Jimmy Barker hooked his left ear with a fishhook, Carol came to the rescue. She freed him from the barbs while three strong uncles held him down. His howls echoed off the mountains and brought many neighbors running.

There also was the time that Bev Middleton spilled a whole pot of hot barley soup in her lap. Carol treated her with ointment from her big, brown medical bag. Soon Bev was good as new. She threw away the checkered apron she'd been wearing, though, declaring it bad luck. A stray dog found the apron a few days later and, believe it or not, returned it to Bev's front door. Bev decided it wasn't such bad luck after all and cleaned it up. She wore it for years without ever spilling hot soup on it again.

Then there was the time Addison Clay needed a bad tooth pulled. He wouldn't go to Seward, so Izzy and Smokey got a hold of him while Carol yanked the tooth out with a pair of alcohol-soaked needle-nose pliers. Addison was already fairly alcohol soaked at the time, which helped a lot.

One glorious June day, old man Snyder, a sourdough from way back, came to Carol with a problem. He was constipated and feeling mighty poorly. Carol mixed up some warm, soapy water and poured it into a gallon tin can that had a hose attached — she kept that contraption around for the occasional enema emergency. She gave it to Snyder and told him to go to the outhouse and take care of business.

Snyder was gone for a long time. Carol began to worry. After nearly an hour had passed, she decided to check on her patient.

"How are you doing in there?" she hollered. "What's taking so long?"

"Well," drawled Snyder from the privy. "It takes a while to drink all this nasty stuff through this little bitty hose!"

I wager he was blowing bubbles for a week.

Carol sure had enough to keep her busy, and we were grateful to have a such a good nurse in our midst.

Besides being our only medical person, Carol also was my best friend. Although nearly a decade older than me, she didn't look it.

I'd kinda let myself go, scorning makeup and letting my gray hairs accumulate. And I never passed up a piece of pie or a slab of home-baked bread with peanut butter.

Carol, on the other hand, tinted her permed hair every month and always gussied up with a touch of lipstick and powder. She experimented with various diets found in the *Ladies Home Journal* and kept her svelte figure.

I imagine we looked like the number 10 as we walked along together — she tall and thin, me short and round. Widowed many years, Carol had a grown son and a daughter in Spokane. She was a grandmother several times over, and although she rarely saw her family, she was proud of them all and exchanged letters frequently.

Carol came to Alaska to work for a few years at the hospital in Seward back in the late '30s. She discovered Muckluck while on a fishing trip and liked what she saw. Since she'd put aside enough money from her husband's insurance and her nurse's salary to live comfortably, she moved lock, stock and barrel to Muckluck and never regretted it for a minute. She quickly learned to live off the land — and the edible goodies folks often gave her as payment for her medical services.

Everyone loved Carol. And while most folks have a story or two to tell of how she came to their rescue during bouts of flu, measles or mumps — or how she bound up their wounds and soothed their fevered brows — I remember her fun side.

~ 7 ~

What I found most captivating about Carol was her wicked sense of humor and willingness to try anything within reason. And sometimes without reason. Carol was a real kick in the pants.

Once when the blueberries were ripe on the mountainside, Carol and I decided to spend an afternoon at our favorite berry patch about two miles north of town. We sat on our fannies to pick berries while enjoying the scenery and each other's company. The sun was warm, the temperature hovering around 75 degrees. When our pails were full, we looked longingly at a small mountain lake nearby. We knew it still would be glacier cold, but it was gloriously blue and tempting, and we were dirty and sweaty.

"Let's do it," Carol said. "Last one in's a dirty, rotten wolverine!"

After shedding our clothes, we raced, buck naked, giggling like schoolgirls toward the lake. We dove right in, screaming as the frigid water caught our breath. And there we were — two middle-age women, splashing and yelling like kids.

We quickly cooled off and climbed, shivering, onto the mossy shore. We laid on the bank, nude as Eve in Eden, soaking up the sun that warmed our winter-white bodies. We chatted drowsily for a while.

"Maybe we'll get a tan," was the last I heard before I dozed off.

We were rudely awakened by the sound of male laughter. We jerked up, doing our best to cover our bits and pieces, and turned sheepishly toward the berry patch where we'd left our clothing.

There stood Bud Reeves, the game warden from Seward. Next to him, wearing my bra over his flannel shirt, was Izzy Fitzheimer. Izzy and Benny Carson, my next-door neighbor, were doubled up laughing their fool heads off while waving our clothes in the air.

33

There was nothing to do but dive back into the water and duck down as far as we could. The men, knowing we were courting hypothermia, chose to be gentlemen. They yelled hearty "Goodbyes," and still roaring with laughter, turned their backs and headed down the mountain toward Muckluck — taking our full berry pails with them. We were plenty mad, and even more embarrassed, but grateful that they had left our clothes behind.

We were the talk of the town for the next few weeks. With my head held high, and as much dignity as I could muster, I rode the wave of infamy until folks grew tired of our little peep show and moved on to talk about other matters.

That's the kind of trouble Carol would get me into. She didn't seem to mind the incident near as much as I did. But Carol, being a nurse, was blasé about the human body and not as persnickety as me. She also looked a heck of a lot better in the buff than I did. She just laughed the whole thing off with a toss of her tinted curls. Those men had sense enough not to say a single word about it to me. They knew I had a hot temper and the muscle to back it up.

Speaking of Carol and me getting into trouble, I remember another time when we went moose hunting. We often hunted together and were pretty good shots. That particular fall we hiked over toward Resurrection Creek, each of us carrying a 30.06.

It was a chilly, overcast day, so we wore heavy, plaid, wool shirts over our long johns. Then we topped off with all-weather jackets and orange caps. Our shoepacks were lined with felt innersoles, and we wore heavy, knitted socks, too. The going was rough, so we wanted to keep plenty warm.

We trudged around for half a day without seeing anything more interesting than a few rabbits and some spruce hens. It was beginning to look like we might run into rain before we got home. Then suddenly through the trees, brush and stinkweed, we saw a nice, young moose in the distance.

Now Carol was off to my right, and she didn't realize I'd seen the moose, too. So we both shot at the same time. The animal dropped like a lead balloon.

We both ran toward our kill — and were shocked to see that the critter was struggling to get up. As we got closer, we were more horrified to see that one of us had shot the rear end of Mrs. Eversall's Guernsey milk cow. Actually, the bullet had just grazed her rump, so she probably fell down from fright. She was up in a jiffy, looking dazed and insulted.

Carol flashed me a look of despair. I knew why.

Mrs. Eversall was a mean old widow lady who'd put up a log shack out in the woods near the creek years before. Nobody bothered to question her right to build it. We didn't know where she came from, or where she got that cow or a skinny goat that roamed around her place at will.

Why did Bossy have to pick that day to wander off the widow's property and into our crosshairs? Dang it all!

We knew we'd have to return the wayward old gal to Mrs. Eversall, and we knew Mrs. E would not be pleased. She didn't like to be disturbed, and she would not be happy to see the wound on Bossy's butt. That cow was her baby.

But being good Muckluckers, we had to do the right thing.

Carol always carried a length of rope when hunting in order to hang the "kill" from a tree to bleed out. So we tied the rope around the cow's neck and led her home, limping through the drizzling rain and fast-falling darkness.

Sure enough, Mrs. Eversall gave us a royal cussing out when we admitted we'd been "dumb enough to mistake a cow for a moose." We let her vent her spleen for a while, knowing it would do her good.

We apologized several times. Carol even offered to patch up the wound. But Mrs. E ordered us to leave, with a couple choice opinions about our parentage and brandishing a red-handled hatchet. The hatchet was very convincing.

You might know, the next time she came to Muckluck Mrs. Eversall told Molly over at the post office that we'd shot her cow. Before long, Carol and I were the town's entertainment. Again. Well, somebody had to be, I guess.

Another incident that comes to mind was the Halloween we decided to go trick-or-treating. Halloween was a big deal with the Muckluck kids, who didn't often get the chance to dress up and go begging for sweets.

There only were a few dozen kids in our little town, but they were a force to be reckoned with at Halloween. Homeowners knew that if they didn't shell out the treats, they were going to get a trick. So residents were prepared when October 31 rolled around. Bing Sultz stocked extra candy at the store, mothers baked cookies and cupcakes and some even made popcorn balls. Single men had coins handy in lieu of edibles.

Carol thought it would be fun to don costumes and do some door-to-door panhandling ourselves. I was doubtful at first, but she talked me into it, as always. After rumaging through crates of long-outdated clothes and a rag bag, Carol came up with a pretty passable get-up made from an old fur coat. She decided to be a teddy bear. She stuffed the hand-stitched costume with a few pillows, made a mask out of papier-mâché and then tied a blue ribbon around her neck. Teddy was ready.

I, lacking Carol's creativity and resources, threw together a hobo outfit. I tied a kerchief around a bundle on a stick — the finished product, in my day, was known as a bindle — and shoved my hair under a fedora that had belonged to my late father. With a touch of charcoal to create a scrubby beard, I looked like many of the local fellas. Scruffy. Only the bindle identified me as a hobo.

We set off as soon as it was dark and easily mingled with a few town kids dressed as ghosts, witches, pirates and a few unidentified characters. We chose to trick-or-treat with the younger kids, because we didn't want to get mixed up in any pranks that older kids pulled, like "toilet tipping."

Toilet tipping, which usually was done late at night, was guaranteed to make someone's life miserable. Imagine racing to your outhouse, in the dark, to do your business — only to find your privy tipped on its back and a nasty, gaping hole stinking to high heaven.

We scurried from house to house with the childen, and the townspeople tossed candy and goodies into our bags. Our costumes were a success.

After a couple of hours, our pack of kidlets had to head for their homes. The night belonged to the teddy bear and the hobo. But with our flour sacks full, and my feet throbbing from the oversized shoes I'd worn, I ached to call it quits, too.

Carol, however, wanted to stop at Addison Clay's place to see if we could fool him.

There was no hope of a treat from Addison. He was the town grump — even more so than Mrs. Eversall. But I'd always loved the old crab. When I was a kid, he was very kind to me. He taught me to tie fishing flies and how to whistle with a blade of grass between my thumbs. He showed me how to skip a flat rock across the lake and how to row in his little skiff. We were an odd couple of pals, who never talked much, but just enjoyed being together.

Carol said if Addison didn't come to the door and give us a treat, we would give him a trick. We'd smear his windows with Ivory soap, a bar of which she had concealed inside her costume.

I was reluctant. I hated to bother the old guy. My better sense told me to turn around and head for home, but Carol was feeling frisky and dragged me up to Addison's doorstep.

She banged on the door with her paw, but got no response. Then she kicked the door. We waited. He was in there. We heard him moving around in the dark.

"Come on," Carol whispered when her patience ran out. "Let's get the windows — they need a good cleaning."

Carol had lost her blue ribbon somewhere during the evening's scavenging, so she looked quite authentic as she lumbered over to the front window, bar of Ivory in hand. I, wisely — and cowardly — stayed behind, partially hidden by a cottonwood tree that seemed to grow out of the porch.

As Carol approached the window, the door burst open with a loud crash and Addison came tearing out with a rifle in his hands. Wearing nothing but a ratty nightshirt, which flapped about his knobby knees, he aimed the gun at Carol, who was merrily scrubbing away at the window. Addison's old eyes, dimmed by cataracts, convinced him there was a brown bear on his porch that was trying to break through the window.

Luckily, I was close enough to tackle him just as the gun exploded with a roar. The bullet harmlessly crashed through the porch floorboards.

Addison and I tussled for a while before he became winded, gave up and lay in a fetal position with his hands clasped over his face. I picked up the rifle and placed it out of harm's way.

Carol and I rushed to comfort the old man, who was huffing and slobbering. We tried to convince him he was not being attacked by a bear and a tramp. It took some doing to calm him, but he finally recognized me.

We got him on his feet and into the cabin, then wrapped him in a blanket, lit the lamp and fixed him a cup of tea generously laced with whiskey. We were darned lucky that night that Addison didn't have a heart attack — and didn't turn Carol into a bearskin rug.

Addison was so thankful to be alive, and not a murderer, that he forgot to yell at us. We finally made our apologies and slunk off to our respective homes, thoroughly ashamed of ourselves.

We never went trick-or-treating again. When Addison died, I wrote a poem about him.

Addison Clay

Long ago and far away
My best friend was Addison Clay.
He lived alone and people say
He always declared he liked it that way.

He shack was a hovel, his yard was a mess.
But that's just the way he liked it, I guess.
His wife had long left him for gentler places
And kinder companions with smiles on their faces.

As years slid past slowly and time took its toll
Old Addison Clay grew more lost in his soul.
He smoked like a chimney and drank like a fish.
To be left to himself was his petulant wish.

And then one day sudden old Addison died.
But nobody missed him, and nobody cried
Except one young woman who lived in the town.
She came to the graveyard, and with eyes cast down

She whispered a prayer heard only by God.
She prayed for the soul of that miserable clod.
She said, "God, I know he was mean as a snake
But he was Your child and I ask You to take

Him to someplace that's nice, filled with comfort and light
Where Addison Clay will find peace without fright.
In the hardest of hearts there's some decency,
And although he looked mean, he was kindly to me.

For he was my friend, and he weren't all that bad.
And I was the only friend Addison had.
Born in poverty and strife, never knowing his pa,
Filth and sin and ugliness was all he ever saw.

When he grew up he went to war and learned to kill and hate.
The things he saw tormented him and sealed his bitter fate.
When he came back, his home was gone and work could not be found
And not a single human being would help him off the ground.

So he withdrew from everyone and didn't trust no man.
But he trusted You, he told me true, so I hope you'll understand.
I kneel alone on this windy hill beside his lonely grave
To ask You in Your mercy to take him. To comfort and save

Old Addison Clay who's lying here. He never asked for much.
Please take him to Heaven to be with You — just heal him with Your touch.
And let him know when you see him as he shuffles so slowly your way
That somebody loves him and mourns him, and misses old Addison Clay."

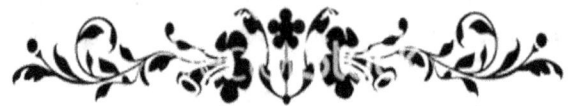

~ 8 ~

The day finally arrived when Benny Carson decided he needed a wife. Word around town was that he'd been subscribing to magazines advertising "mail order brides."

This practice was not unusual in Alaska during the early days, and it still may go on as far as I know. It's not something I'd recommend though, unless one is truly desperate — and even then, it's pretty dicey. I mean, who knows what you might end up with. Could be a serial killer, a lunatic or a politician, God forbid. It's just not the best idea.

But that didn't stop Benny. He took his time leafing through the magazines and finally narrowed the field to a dozen would-be brides. His taste ran toward green-eyed blondes, which whittled the field considerably. He found twelve possibilities and wrote to each of them.

Molly, at the post office, saw that each envelope was carefully printed in pencil. She also noticed that the envelopes he got in return often were colorful and smelled faintly of cologne. Of course, Molly never breathed a word of this to anyone — after all, she was the postmaster. But years later, she confessed to me that she sometimes "couldn't help but notice" certain irregularities that came through the mail.

Correspondence went back and forth for several months before Benny came to my place one afternoon with a handful of letters. He wanted an opinion from a disinterested party.

Disinterested? Heck — I was knee-deep in interest!

"Kate," he whispered, as he looked around furtively to see if anybody else was within earshot. "I need some help here. I've picked the three most likely candidates out of the pack, but I can't make a final decision."

He handed me his bundle of letters.

"I want you to read their letters, look at their pictures, and help me choose," he said.

I was extremely flattered by the trust Benny had in my judgment, but I also was somewhat concerned at the awesome responsibility being thrust upon me.

"Benny, are you sure you want me to read these letters?" I asked.

"Yup, I'm sure," he said. "I'll go back home while you read through 'em, and then you can tell me what you think."

Benny darted out the door and was gone before I could argue.

I've gotta tell you, those letters were something. Each woman described herself in glowing terms. And each claimed to have green eyes and blonde hair, which was impossible to tell from the black and white photos, and were nineteen to thirty-four years old.

So far so good. A couple, at least, were in Benny's age range. Since he was thirty-six, I discarded the nineteen-year-old early on and concentrated on the two remaining gals.

Miss Madeline O'Reilly, twenty-nine, never married and worked as a waitress in a family restaurant in Rochester, Minnesota. She looked quite presentable in her photograph and wrote that she enjoyed winter sports, such as skiing, skating and sledding. Her hobbies included knitting and wrestling.

Hmm, that gave me pause for thought. Quite the contrast. Miss O'Reilly closed her letter with: "May God bless you, dear man."

The second lady, Betsy Deaver, wrote that she was thirty-three, a widow for five years and owned a small farm in Colorado. Her letter stated she was tired of trying to keep the farm afloat and gladly would sell it and move to a "more interesting part of the world."

She didn't seem to have time for hobbies but claimed to be a "real fine cook" and liked to cuddle. She looked pleasant, if somewhat tired, in the photo she enclosed.

Now I was in a pickle. Both women looked promising. But what if I chose the wrong one and stuck Benny with a lemon? He

42

was a good guy and a fine neighbor, so I felt the weight of my decision heavy on my shoulders.

I sat and reread the letters several times. I kept pairing each letter with its writer's picture. I pondered and wavered back and forth until my head began to throb.

After several hours, Benny came knocking again, wondering what was taking me so long.

"I just can't make up my mind, Ben," I admitted. "Which one do you feel best about?"

And wouldn't you know — he pointed straight to the picture of the nineteen-year-old! I shoulda guessed.

I voiced my concerns about the age difference, and the inexperience of such a young girl. But Benny stood firm. I got the impression he hadn't so much wanted my opinion as my agreement with his selection. So I read her letter and tried real hard to see her from Benny's viewpoint.

Miss Violet Gardner, an orphan since the age of six, was raised in a children's shelter in Salem, Oregon. She'd finished high school and worked as a nanny for a well-to-do timber family in Eugene. Her duties included light cooking, cleaning and laundry for five kids. She wrote that she didn't expect much in the way of fancy do-dads, but that she was looking for a good, God-fearing man who would treat her well and give her a child or two of her own. Her picture showed a solemn, sweet-faced girl, of average size, with enormous, wistful eyes. I might have judged her too quickly.

"Benny, if you want this one, I say you should go get her."

He grabbed the letter out of my hands and was off like a flash to write a proposal to Miss Violet.

Two months later, almost to the day, Izzy Fitzheimer returned from his weekly trip to Seward with a passenger. Benny's bride-to-be had arrived.

Most Muckluckers had heard about the mail order proposal and were eager to make the young lady's acquaintance. We all thought the world of Benny and wished him only the best of luck with his young fiancé.

~ 9 ~

Violet had requested a simple Protestant service, and Father Sorinoff completely understood. Since the preacher from Seward was due any day, we began planning a nice wedding for Benny and Violet.

In the meantime, Violet stayed with me and proved to be a comfortable and pleasant companion. She pitched right in with the cooking and what little cleaning needed to be done. She also confided in me that she found Benny to be "entirely acceptable, and rather handsome." Her shy smile was captivating — but I never saw her laugh.

The women of Muckluck held several coffee klatches to prepare for the wedding and assign chores. Talk about exciting! We hadn't had a wedding in years, especially one where the bride-to-be was content to let us do all the fussing. Violet had brought along a simple white dress for the ceremony. Now it was up to us to add the trimmings, so we formed a wedding committee.

Wilma Moffid stitched up a short veil and adorned it with fabric flowers to make a wreath for Violet's hair. Thelma Ward found wildflowers to make a colorful bouquet, and Carol came through with a blue garter sprinkled with rhinestones. We didn't ask.

Esther Waldorf rounded up a few Native prayers, which she translated into English, and Nell Dodson, blessed with a lovely contralto voice, offered to sing "Oh Promise Me" and "Because."

Bev Middleton said she'd bake a four-tier wedding cake, with raspberry jelly filling, and a large flat cake for the reception. And Val Sultz found a case of punch over at the store just waiting for an occasion.

We also threw a wedding shower and gave the new couple many useful gifts. We felt we had covered the bases.

Violet was quietly delighted with all the attention and preparations. She then asked me to be her maid of honor.

At first I politely demurred. I only owned one dress, and it was completely out of style. I felt ill-suited, especially with my tomboy appearance, to serve as maid of anything.

But Violet stood firm. And since she asked so little, I agreed to serve as best I could. Nell, who was built somewhat on the same stocky lines as me, offered up a wild rose-colored gown with matching shoes. They pinched a bit, but they were wearable.

Benny made a quick trip to Seward, where he purchased a brown wool suit that had been on the rack at Urbach's men's store for at least a dozen years. There were few suits to choose from, so it had to fill the bill. Carol made a few alterations to the suit and hemmed the pant legs. The groom-to-be actually gussied up quite handsomely.

When we heard that Reverend Sneed would arrive on July 15, the wedding plans roared into high gear. We had a deadline to meet.

The wedding day dawned bright and warm. The ladies brought out their finest dresses and coaxed their men into their best duds. Benny's best man, Bud Reeves, wore his game warden uniform, which, in my opinion, made him look not only toothsome, but official, too.

I helped Violet dress and then pinned up her hair, while the rest of the wedding committee set about their appointed tasks. Muckluck buzzed like bees around honey. I can't remember seeing such a hustle-bustle before or since.

Violet and Benny chose the banks of Moose Run as their wedding site. The creek ran smooth and melodious, sun shining like diamonds on its surface. Every once in a while a trout leapt out of the water, then fell back into the stream with a resounding splash. Soft breezes rustled the trees and fireweed, helping to keep the mosquitoes and no-see-ums at bay.

The bridal couple, myself and Bud lined up in front of Reverend Sneed, with our backs to the assembled townsfolk.

Then the reverend, standing with his back to the creek, began the ceremony by welcoming everyone and asking if anyone had an objection to the couple being joined in Holy matrimony. A moment of silence followed, and then all heck broke loose.

Benny's Siberian husky, Sampson, tore barking through the crowd, hell-bent on reaching the honorable reverend.

You see, every time the reverend came to hold services in Muckluck, he'd bring along a big knuckle bone for Sampson, who often was tied to a tree in front of Benny's place. The preacher was a little intimidated by Sampson, and he just wanted to stay on the dog's good side.

On that day, however, he had a lot on his mind and had forgotten the bone. But Sampson did not forget. When the husky heard the voice of his favorite treat provider, he lunged free of his rope and galloped to get his bone.

Sampson zigzagged between the bride and groom and jumped straight onto Reverend Sneed's chest, knocking the Holy man backward into Moose Run.

Fortunately, the water there was shallow. The reverend sat up, stunned and a bit terrified, as the huge dog licked his face and nosed his pockets looking for his treat. Reverend Sneed tried to push Sampson away with one hand, while he held his Bible high and dry above his head with the other.

For a second or two there was complete silence. Then Violet began to laugh. She laughed long and loud, while tears rolled down her cheeks and her face glowed beet red.

Benny, as surprised at Violet's laughter as he was at seeing Sampson atop Reverend Sneed, grasped Violet to his chest and began laughing, too. Soon everyone was doubled over laughing to beat the band, choking and snorting.

Bud and Olav, our two law officers, recovered first and waded into the water. Bud pulled the dog off, while Olav plucked the preacher out of the creek and stood him back on dry land.

It took some time for everyone to stop laughing — and then we didn't know what to do. We just kinda stood around with our heads down, embarrassed-like, shuffling our feet and wringing our hands. Ever so often Violet would let out a muffled giggle, causing Benny's shoulders to shake, but he kept his dignity pretty well, all things considered.

Reverend Sneed, to his everlasting credit, wiped dog drool off his face and glasses, shook himself mightily, and then returned to the task at hand. One of the Raben twins dragged the disappointed Sampson home.

"Dearly beloved," the reverend intoned, and we set off again to join Violet and Benny as husband and wife. It was a lovely ceremony. People still were wiping their eyes when Mr. and Mrs. Benny Carson turned to greet their well-wishers.

The reception was beautiful. All our preparations paid off, and that part of the shindig went off without a hitch. As the sun set behind Bald Mountain, the newlyweds retired to Benny's cabin for the night. But not to sleep.

I probably should explain about a shivaree before I go on. I think the custom is as old as the Middle Ages. Maybe older. Though I certainly won't swear to it. Sadly, I don't think the practice is enjoyed any longer. People today are too interested in their television shows and all the playthings technology has invented to keep them entertained. They don't know how to have real fun with their friends and neighbors.

But back in the olden days, and even in Alaska in the 1940s, a shivaree following a wedding was an absolute necessity. It was about as much fun as anyone could stand.

It always started about the time the newly married couple prepared for bed. A bunch of the town folks would arrived at the newlywed's door, singing and banging on tin pie plates and making all kinds of noise. This was supposed to distract the bride and groom from their own private party.

The racket would continue until the husband and wife opened the door, and either invited the crowd in, or offered some form of refreshment. It could be dangerous to open the door, though, as there had been times when some of the more mischievous young fellas had "kidnapped" the bride and hid her until the groom found and claimed her again. We women didn't care for that aspect of the shivaree, so it wasn't often practiced in Muckluck — though you just never knew. Caution was the rule for newlyweds.

Anyway, the night of Violet and Benny's nuptials, a gang of us snuck up to their door and let go with the loudest racket you ever heard. We whooped and hollered and nearly blew our own eardrums out for half an hour.

But nobody came to the door. The shades were drawn over the windows, and no light shown through cracks between the logs. We finally decided that the Carsons were not going to open up.

Felix went and knocked on the door. When he got no response, he tentatively tried the door knob. The door creaked open. We craned our necks to see into the darkness. Those in the back began to push, and pretty soon, Felix and some of the others were inside. The cabin was empty.

The joke was on us. Benny, one of the worst shivaree offenders in the past, had anticipated our nighttime serenade. He pitched a tent in the woods the day before the wedding, complete with mosquito netting, flowers and candles. He and Violet slipped out while the rest of us were packing up the reception debris. It's to be assumed that they had a peaceful and romantic night among the flora and fauna of Alaska's wilderness. We never asked.

The marriage was a huge success. The Carsons eventually had six little ones and built a larger house. Benny was a devoted and loving husband and father. In his spare time, he wrote a book about a mad scientist. It became a best seller, so he wrote a dozen or so more. Violet proved to be the cream of the crop where mail-order brides were concerned.

Some of their children went Outside to college — one became a psychiatrist, a daughter became an airline pilot and one son wrote for movies in Hollywood. The rest of the kids stayed in Muckluck and provided Violet and Benny with a whole truckload of grandbabies. I am the proud Godmother to several Carsons who were, and are, a great blessing to me.

Everlasting Love

I could not ever write enough
To tell of all my love.
For it is countless as the stars
That shine in heaven above.

I love you for the many things
You are — and mean to me.
I love you, Dear, because you hold
And shape my destiny.

I love your strength and faithfulness,
I love your honesty.
I love you for the many things
One cannot touch or see.

I love you for your tenderness,
The way you think of me
Before you think about yourself
The way true love should be.

I love you when you hold me tight
And kiss away my tears.
For you make everything all right
And banish all my fears.

I love you for you're always there
Beside me when I call.
And of all the things I know and love
I love you most of all.

~ 10 ~

I hate to admit it, but we once had a thief in Muckluck. After many years enjoying crime-free living, we found ourselves in the midst of a genuine crime spree.

It all started when a stranger came to town and rented a room from Bing Sultz in back of his store. Bing had been using the enclosed back porch, which the Natives called a calidor, to store extra tinned goods, cans of gasoline and animal pelts. But he figured he could store all that stuff somewhere else if it meant getting a paying tenent.

Besides that, Val had been complaining bitterly about the stench from pelts and animal parts hanging in that storage area.

You see, for some predatory animals there was a bounty to be had if you mailed certain parts — like the right front paw — to fish and wildlife folks in Juneau. For other animals, maybe in an effort to reduce their population, only the males could be killed. To insure the correct sex, and collect the bounty, dried testicles were sent to Juneau.

These sorts of body parts were stored in the Sultz's calidor, which is where people generally stored everything from slabs of bacon to snowshoes. Bing had nailed paws and testicles to the rafters, where they added considerably to the aroma of the place. With the arrival of a paying guest, Bing gathered up the offending animal doohickeys and shipped them off to the state capital, much to Val's relief.

Bing explained the lingering odor to his tenant, Orvill Nivens. Orvill said the smell didn't bother him much. He planned to air out the place and was sure he'd get used to it anyway.

Both parties were happy with the arrangement. Bing and Val were glad to have the extra income, and Orvill had a snug little room to call home.

So all was well for a month or so. Orvill was a quiet, keep-to-yourself kind of man who took his meals with the Sultz family. Otherwise, he stayed out of sight.

Then, one day things started disappearing.

The first to complain that she'd misplaced her mother's fake diamond ring was Wilma Moffid. It wasn't worth a lot of money, but it had sentimental value. Wilma was quite attached to it. She searched their place high and low for days, but the ring didn't turn up. She feared she might have thrown it out with the dishwater, though she usually put it on the counter beside the dishpan when she washed up.

A while later, Father Sorinoff noticed a small, gold cross was missing from his bureau. He always placed the cross on a porcelain saucer, along with other religious items, before he went to bed. When he awoke late one morning, the little medals and icons were there, but the cross was gone.

The schoolhouse was hit next. Thelma had a dozen small, silver spoons she'd collected from various states when she visited Outside. She'd brought them to the school to show the kids and forgot to take them home for several days. Then two of them went missing. Thelma hated to think any of her students had taken them, and they all swore sacred oaths that they definitely had not. Gazing at their sad eyes and honest round faces, she believed them.

Although a mystery, not too much thought was given to the missing items. They easily could have been misplaced.

But then I had a visit from the thief. And I knew darn good and well that I hadn't misplaced anything.

My father had left me a solid-gold medallion on a gold nugget chain. He had used it as a watch fob when they were in fashion. I hung it on a nail on the wall where I could see it every day.

One day it simply wasn't there. I knew I hadn't moved it, and it sure didn't jump off that nail all by itself. So I hiked, fuming, over to Olav's place to report the theft.

Olav had spent most of the summer working at a cannery over on Cook Inlet near Kenai, but he checked in from time to time to make sure all was well with his town. Since nothing much ever happened in Muckluck to require his lawman services, he came home only occasionally to pick up his mail or some supplies.

It just so happened that Olav was home that day. He'd been preparing to return to Kenai when he heard about Thelma's disappearing spoons. She also told him that Wilma was missing a ring and Father Sorinoff was short a gold cross. Added to my recent loss, this looked like serious business — a regular crime wave.

We pondered about it for a while over cups of thick, black coffee. Then we heard a knock. When Olav opened his cabin door, there stood Val, wringing her hands, and Bing looking quite angry.

Bing told us that he'd left some fishing gear out to dry on the back porch, and now his favorite lure was gone. He said he first thought Val had taken it out of spite, since she wasn't real happy about being left alone to tend the store while he made frequent trips to Moose Run to dip a line.

But, Bing said, after Val hotly denied the dirty deed, he threatened to tell Olav about the theft. That's when Val yelled, "Let's go!"

And there they were, both mad as wet hens.

Olav calmed them with cups of strong coffee, and we four began, as they call it these days, to brainstorm. We all knew everybody in town and had known them for years. With the exception of Violet, Benny's recent bride. But we eliminated her without a blink.

Then Val had a thought. They had a boarder at the store — Mr. Orvill Nivens. Nobody knew a thing about him, except that he'd appeared suddenly with very few belongings. He stayed to himself and was closed-mouthed, just the way you'd want a boarder to be.

But there was something suspicious about him, too. He went off into the woods every morning after breakfast and was gone until dinner time.

Olav returned to the store with the Sultzes and banged on the tenant's door. At first there was no answer, but then the door slowly opened a crack. Mr. Orvill Nivens poked his nose out. He recognized the marshal and stepped outside.

"What's going on?" he asked.

"I wonder if I could come in for a minute and talk to you," Olav said.

"I'd rather talk out here," replied Orvill.

"Well then, I guess I'll just have to insist on stepping inside, since this is technically Sultz's place, and they've given me permission," Olav said.

So they went inside, and Olav took a good look around. He didn't see any of the missing objects, but he did see some unusual stuff, including bits of moss, leaves, vines and various kinds of weeds. Well, there was no law against having junk like that laying around, so Olav had no cause to arrest Orvill.

But the marshal felt in his bones that something was amiss, so he came up with an idea. He invited Orvill to come stay at his place for a few days while he, Olav, gave more thought on the matter.

At first Orvill refused flat out, but after Olav said he thought he'd be within his rights to restrain him "on suspicion" so to speak, Orvill sighed, grabbed a clean shirt and his toothbrush, and went to Olav's cabin. I understand they were not the best of roommates, but they made do.

For a couple of days, Orvill just sulked. He wouldn't talk, so Olav left him alone. Finally, Orvill asked if he could go for a walk. After Orvill promised on a Bible that he'd return, Olav, a trusting soul who had no real cause to keep Orvill locked up, let him go.

"You just be back by supper time — we're having moose stew," Olav said, in an attempt to lure Orvill back to the cabin.

Orvill kept his promise, and soon the marshal was letting him go for walks alone on a regular basis.

One day, while enjoying his new-found freedom, Orvill noticed something interesting in the woods. I must explain at this point that Orvill was somewhat of an amateur botanist. He was in Alaska collecting specimens of various plant life for his collection, and at the same time, taking note of our local feathered friends.

That day he saw a jay bird sitting on a branch, eyeing something on Molly Parkins' front porch. It happened to be a three-penny nail. Orvill stood perfectly still, unnoticed by the jay. He watched the bird swoop down, snatch the nail in his beak and fly off into the woods. Orvill quietly followed and soon saw the jay land in the branches of an old spruce tree. The bird stayed for only a minute, and then flew off again.

"Aha," Orvill says to himself. "Gray jays also are known as camp robbers, and I do believe I've found myself our thief!"

He rushed back to the cabin to tell Olav. The two of them then hustled off to the old spruce. Along the way, they collected one of the Waldorf kids, young Ralphie, who was known for his skill in climbing. When the trio arrived at the tree, Ralphie scampered up its prickly branches until he was about three-quarters of the way up.

"Oh my gosh! Ralphie yelled. "You'll never believe what I found."

"Give us a hint," coaxed Olav wryly.

"Well, it's a camp robber's nest all right … and it's full of stuff," Ralphie exclaimed excitedly, choosing not to play guessing games.

"Can you bring 'er down?" asked Orvill.

"Sure," Ralphie said. He carefully returned to earth with the nest in hand.

Inside were a small cross, a ring, a gold watch fob, a fishing lure, a three-penny nail, two small spoons and a silver hatpin that nobody had reported missing. Orvill had "caught" the thief and cleared his good name at the same time.

Camp robbers usually steal bits of food, but they can't turn down shiny little doodads, either. A real dedicated camp robber will even enter a home or building through an open window and help himself to a goodie. Since the weather had been so cooperative, most of us left our windows open day and night. Easy access for a thief.

Everyone was thrilled to get their belongings back. After many apologies were offered, and graciously accepted by Orvill, the botanist was declared a bona-fide hero, and the case was officially closed.

~ 11 ~

Are you tired of my stories yet? No? You want to hear more about Muckluck? Well, then, have some more sweet tea and I'll just dredge up a couple more for you.

I remember a particularly dry summer. No rain fell at all, which didn't bother the trees and larger bushes, but it did cause the grass and weeds to wilt and turn brown. Even Moose Run was low, since the winter before had not seen much snow. I don't recall the exact year, but think it was in the early '40s.

Folks hauled water from the creek or hoisted it from their wells, if they had one. Everyone needed water to drink, cook and keep their gardens. That summer the road through town was dusty, and so were our residents.

There weren't as many mosquitoes as usual, but the no-see-ums were fierce. We went around with gobs of baking soda paste dotting our faces, necks and arms in an effort to calm the itching. No-see-ums tend to take a chunk right out of you, so I assume they bite rather than sting.

One day, around 2:30 p.m., three shots rang out — one right after the other. That was the signal for trouble. Big trouble. Muckluckers dropped what they were doing and ran out into the road to find out what was happening. Then they smelled smoke.

"Fire!" someone hollered. "There's a fire over at the church!"

The word was yelled from person to person. Soon folks were stampeding from every direction as they grabbed buckets, pails and dishpans. They then raced to the river, filled their containers and headed to the church. Men, women and children all knew they might not only lose their beloved Russian church, but if the fire spread, their homes, too.

I'll admit it. There was panic a-plenty. I ran alongside Benny, who had not yet sent for and married Violet. He swung two large

55

buckets as he ran. I lugged my drinking water pail. Soon we joined a line of folks passing full containers of water from the creek to the church. As soon as a bucket was passed inside the church and emptied, it was handed back along the line and returned to the creek. A constant bucket brigade kept the flow of water steady.

Only Father Sorinoff and a few of the men knew what was burning inside the church. The rest of us only knew that whatever it was, it had to be extinguished immediately. Gospodi pomilui!

Through exhaustion and breaking backs, we kept those buckets moving back and forth from the river to the church. Our arms felt like lead. We coughed and spit and grumbled, but we kept those buckets going.

Finally Father Sorinoff and a few men came out the front door and said the fire was out. Actually, it had not been in the church at all, but in the shed that had housed our dead stranger. The shed was near the back of the church, but due to the fast response to the shots with our bucket brigade, the church only suffered a bit of smoke damage, along with some mud tracked inside by the firefighters. The shed, however, was a total loss. It had been made of old, dry wood, and went up like a tinder box.

We all wearily trooped around to see the sad remains — a heap of wet, black ashes, cinders, sludge and a few glowing embers that were quickly doused. Nobody seemed to know what had started the fire, and we were too tired to worry about it. Shaking our heads, we trudged back to our homes, leaving a few fellas to make sure there were no flare ups.

"Have you seen my Archie?" Amelia Eades yelled at me as I neared home. "I didn't see him at the church. I can't find him."

Amelia looked a wreck and sounded worried. Archie, her middle child, was in the second grade. He was probably about seven years old.

"I know I'm being silly, but I'm really scared," she said. "He wouldn't miss a big deal like a fire."

I could see Amelia's legs shaking. Her fingers clenched and unclenched as she tried to get hold of herself.

"No, Amelia, I haven't seen him for a couple of days," I said. "Let's get some more folks and start looking for him. He'll turn up real soon, I'm sure."

I meant to sound confident, but tears continued to run down her soot-streaked face. I felt a lump in my throat. Nothing is worse than a lost child.

And so began the second heart-stopper of the day. Before long, most everyone in town knew little Archie was missing. Some of us had a really bad feeling in our bellies that maybe he had been in that shed and perished in the fire. We didn't want to even think about it, but it was a possibility.

Several men took a closer look at the remains of the shed, but with piles of debris still smoldering, they really couldn't see all that well. They didn't want to see what they were afraid they might see.

The rest of us searched high and low throughout the town. Some of the older kids went into the woods and beat the bushes for hours. The rest of us hollered until our throats were parched. Suppertime came and went, but nobody went home to eat. We searched until we figured we'd covered every square inch of Muckluck. And then some.

Amelia was exhaused. Her other two children hung onto her like they were afraid she'd disappear, too. Her husband, Rupert, was in Anchorage working at the airport that summer, so he was spared the brutal ordeal of hunting for Archie.

We finally had to call it quits for the night. It was fall and the days were getting shorter. Feeling sad and guilty, Muckluckers dropped out of the hunt one by one and returned to their homes.

Eventually only Amelia, her kids, Carol and I were left standing alone near the church.

"He couldn't be in there … he just couldn't be in there," Amelia whispered. Her voice was almost gone from yelling and crying.

Carol suggested we take Amelia and her children to their home and get them to eat something before putting them to bed. As exhausted as we all were, we knew it was the right thing to do. And Amelia didn't argue, she just picked up little Sadie, took Theo by the hand and headed for home. Carol and I followed, barely able to put one foot in front of the other.

We heated up some Campbell's soup and made toast with peanut butter. The kids ate some, but Amelia just sat with her head in her hands. Once in a while she sipped at a cup of coffee. Carol and I washed up the kids and put them into their p.j.'s.

"You know," Amelia whispered, "I'd really like to say a prayer."

That suited us fine. We had been praying silently all day, but Amelia wanted an "out loud" prayer. She asked me to say it. All of us bowed our heads and folded our hands.

"Dear Lord," I prayed, "please help us find Archie real soon. Please let him be safe and well. You know he's just a little fella, so we ask that your angels be around him wherever he is, and let him not be afraid. We pray for Amelia and her kids that you will comfort them and give them peace and rest. In Your name we pray, Amen."

"Amen," everyone chorused.

It was pretty pitiful as prayers go, but it was the best I could muster on short notice. It seemed to satisfy Amelia.

While Amelia went to her room to rest, Carol and I tucked Sadie and Theo into their beds. Theo cried when he saw the empty place where Archie had slept all his life. When Sadie saw Theo crying, she started in, too. Soon all four of us were sobbing and hugging.

Right in the middle of blowing my nose, I heard a sound coming from under Theo's bed. It sounded like a muffled, slurpy sob.

"Quiet!" I hissed. "Everybody be quiet and quit your bawling."

Carol and the children stopped immeditely.

I got down on my weary knees, lifted the bedspread and peeked under the bed. And there he was, all curled up like a potato bug, eyes swimming with tears and shaking like he had the plague.

I reached under and pulled Archie out by his shirt front. Then I clutched him to my chest as hard as I've ever hugged anybody.

"Amelia!" I cried. "Come in here and get your boy."

You can imagine the scene that took place following Archie's discovery. Amelia wanted to hug and kiss and beat the britches off of him all at the same time. She settled for many hugs and kisses and two sharp whacks on the butt, just to make a point.

"Why in Heaven's name didn't you answer when people were yelling your name?"

"Because I was scared," Archie said.

"So why were you hiding in the first place?" his mother wanted to know. Heck, we all wanted to know.

At first Archie stayed mum. Then it all came tumbling out.

"I just wanted to see the shed where that dead man had been. I heard some of the kids saying his ghost is still there, and I wanted to see it. So I took a candle and some matches with me and snuck into the shed and had me a good look around," Archie said. "Then I heard a sound like a ghost, and I dropped the candle and ran for my life."

The little boy's eyes were wide open and brimming with tears that ran down his cheeks, mixed with snot, and continued down off his chin.

"And just what did the ghost sound like?" I asked.

"It made a flapping sort of noise with its sheet and then it asked, 'Who, who, who?' I said, 'I'm Archie Eades', and then I took off and ran back home and hid under the bed. When I heard my name called, I thought it was the ghost after me, so I just kept quiet."

That seemed a reasonable explanation for a seven-year-old who couldn't tell an owl from a ghost. So Carol and I left Archie to his mother's care and went to spread the word that the lost lamb had been found.

That night Amelia thought she was the luckiest mother in the world. And so did we. Before I went to sleep I said another prayer. It was very short — just a heartfelt "thank you."

Now I hate to tell this part of the story, but I said I'd tell the truth about Muckluck, so it's gotta be told.

About two years after Archie's adventure with the "ghost" and the fire at St. Anastasia's, Archie's little sister, Sadie, was playing kick-the-can with some of the bigger kids. Archie said later she was so happy to be included in their game.

The kids said Sadie ran to hide over by Moose Run. She picked a spot where there were big rocks in the creek, and she waded in to hide behind one of them. The water was swift and cold. She slipped and was swept away. We found her little body later that day, her yellow dress with purple butterflies had snagged on a fallen tree limb.

We all took Sadie's passing hard. The whole town was heartbroken. One of our precious children was gone, and there was nothing we could do to bring her back. I think we all felt a little guilty. Like we hadn't kept as careful a watch as we should have. It was terrible.

After the funeral, the Eades family packed up and moved away. They didn't even say goodbye. But we understood. It was just too hard to speak to folks and see the sympathy in their eyes.

I wouldn't want you to think that the Eades' children were bad kids because of Archie's fire and Sadie's death. They were typical kids who hadn't lived long enough to learn the hard lessons of life. They didn't know how quickly the world can turn upside-down, and that one small slip can make the difference between life and death. Sometimes there are second chances. Sometimes not.

The Eades left a forwarding address at the post office, some place in Ohio as I recollect. I sent them a card at Christmas, but nobody ever heard from them again.

Forget-me-nots were planted every spring on Sadie's small grave, too. Just like those on the grave of the stranger who died in my outhouse. Our modest cemetery looked pretty in the summer with yellow dandelions, tall fuchsia fireweed and the sky-blue forget-me-nots.

Carol and I often strolled over there to neaten things up and have a picnic. To my way of thinking, there is no place on earth more peaceful and calming to the soul than a well-tended, well-loved cemetery.

Life's Final Sunset

I walk alone with Jesus
As the sun sinks o'er the crest
Of glowing hills to fall asleep
At last on Heaven's breast.

I walk there with the Master
And I see God's painted world:
The golden hills my pathway fills
The sunset's glow unfurled.

My soul is filled with wonder
As I walk there with my Lord.
The paradise of Eden lies
Before me, splendor-stored.

My Guardian's hand is ready
When the thorns obstruct the way,
And He leads me toward the hilltop
As He's led me through each day.

While He walks along beside me,
He guides me gently through
The sun-drenched paths to glory
Where the skies are always blue.

Then at last I reach the summit
And my feet no longer roam,
For the golden heavens open
And my Savior leads me home.

~ 12 ~

One of our more colorful Muckluckers was Granny Annie. Born Anna Vegoda in Naples, Italy, she came to America as a young woman. She lived with relatives in the Little Italy section of Boston for a while, doing housework and child care for the more affluent Bostonians.

While strolling through Boston Commons one day, near the spot where witches were hanged years ago, she met a charming Irishman, Ned O'Grady. He had hair as red as tomato sauce, snapping blue eyes and a sprinkle of freckles all over his face, hands and arms. He was exotic and irresistible to the dark and lovely Italian girl, and he had that famous Irish "gift of gab." No doubt he had kissed the Blarney Stone a time or two.

Before one could say "leaping leprechauns," the two of them were engaged and then married. Everyone teased that two good Catholics soon would have a houseful of kids. That didn't happen.

The O'Gradys were happy, nevertheless, and they lived and worked in Boston for twenty years. But when Ned heard about Alaska, and the gold that hid, not in a pot at the end of a rainbow, but in the mountains and streams of that great land, he convinced Anna, now known as Annie, to once more leave the comforts of home and travel to the unknown, untamed northland.

Once they arrived in Seward, Ned took a job longshoring on the docks. It was hard work and provided no gold. Annie took in washing to supplement the family income. Still no babies, but happy, the O'Gradys felt they'd made a good decision to move to Alaska.

Annie also learned the hard way that life is unpredictable at best. At worst, it's downright cruel. A cable broke one day, dumping a large crate of machinery parts directly on Ned. He was killed instantly. He was only 57 years old.

Annie was inconsolable. She had no children, no kin and few friends to support her in her grief. Somehow she managed to survive. But she didn't learn to really live again until she discovered Muckluck.

Muckluck folks just had a way of taking strangers to their hearts. Especially strangers who had sad faces and looked like they needed a cup of strong, black coffee, a sympathetic ear to listen, and a soft shoulder to cry on. Annie found it all in Muckluck. She returned to Seward, packed her meager belongings and moved to an abandoned cabin over near the schoolhouse.

Her choice of housing was a good one. She became best friends with Thelma Ward, who in those days was just beginning her long stint as teacher at Muckluck. Through Thelma, Annie met all the school-age kids in town. She became Thelma's assistant, with approval from Juneau, and fell in love with her students.

Annie had her children at last. Lots and lots of children. And they adored her. The kids soon dubbed her Granny Annie, a name she cherished. In time, the rest of the town began calling her Granny Annie, too. She was a treasure for sure.

If you ever got behind on your mending, craved some authentic Italian spaghetti, or just needed a hug, you headed for Granny Annie's place. And you got what you needed. With a cheery "Ciao bambino," and a tight squeeze, you knew you were in a good, warm, safe place. A place that smelled heavenly of oregano, sage, thyme, basil, onion, and best of all, garlic. If you were lucky, and it was baking day, you'd be offered a biscotti, or better yet, a cannoli.

Granny Annie was tiny, but she had a huge personality. She always was smiling or laughing, telling silly little jokes and singing Italian songs. Occasionally, when feeling a tad pensive in memory of Ned, she was known to sing "Danny Boy" or "I'll Take You Home Again, Kathleen." Then she'd wipe her chocolate-brown eyes, fluff up her white puff of hair and get on with business.

One day Granny Annie rode to Seward with Izzy to buy some Italian seasoning. She didn't trust Izzy to get the right kind. While in the "city," she happened to run into the lady she'd worked for when Ned was alive. The woman was very fond of Annie and invited her to stop in for coffee. Since she and Izzy weren't due to head back to Muckluck for several hours, Annie accepted the offer. I don't think I've ever known anybody to turn down a cuppa coffee in Alaska, although there may have been one or two I missed.

Whether by chance or design, Annie's former employer also invited an older gentleman named Rudolph Nielson. Mr. Nielson, a widower, was tall and had a shock of salt-and-pepper colored hair. He also wore horn-rimmed glasses and talked about his travels in Europe. He loved Italy.

Between cups of coffee and fat slices of gooseberry pie, conversation flew and the afternoon passed quickly. Too soon, Izzy was at the door, eager to head back to Muckluck. Mr. Nielson said he'd like to visit Muckluck some day and, of course, Annie invited him to drop in any time.

"Any time" turned out to be the very next week.

Mr. Nielson had a car. He risked it, as well as life and limb, driving the gravel and dirt roads between Seward and Muckluck. The main road was so narrow, that if a driver met another car coming from the opposite direction, one or the other had to back up to a convenient "turn out" and wait for the other to pass.

I recall some drivers slowing nearly to a stop and honking their horns before going around a sharp curve because trees and high weeds obscured oncoming "traffic." But if you did meet another car, you always waved or honked the horn in greeting. And sometimes you both stopped just to chew the fat.

When Mr. Nielson arrived in Muckluck, he found Granny Annie's home and soon was enjoying her usual offerings of Italian hot dishes and desserts. After that, there was no stopping Mr. Nielson. Every few weeks, he visited Granny Annie. Before the year was out, he proposed marriage.

The happy couple decided at their age a long engagement might be foolish — or fatal. So a date was set for a month after the diamond solitaire was placed on Annie's arthritic finger.

The wedding itself was lovely, dignified and held in St. Anastasia's. Father Sorinoff did his best to perform a traditional Catholic ceremony. The residents of Muckluk turned out as you would expect to honor the newlyweds. In respect to their ages, though, no shivaree was held.

But I've gotta tell you about the bachelor party that took place before the wedding.

Granny Annie insisted on throwing the party herself. She didn't say why and, as always, we didn't ask. Although it seemed a tad odd for the bride to throw the bachelor party.

Annie's plan was to surprise Mr. Nielson the last time he came to town before the wedding. She got together with a bunch of Muckluck women and, eyes twinkling with mischief, she brought forth her plan.

She asked several of the women to play the parts of "fancy gals." After all, every bachelor party needs some flair, so we somewhat reluctantly agreed to do our best. I doubt if anybody but Granny Annie could have talked us into it but, before long, we got into the swing of things.

Carol loved the idea. It was right up her alley. She made a costume of a French maid, including a black, full skirt at mid-thigh, a tiny white apron and a little cap atop her red curls. A feather duster completed her outfit.

Schoolteacher Thelma Ward was quite daring in a long, slinky, red gown with a rather daring neckline. A slit almost up to her knees, elbow length gloves and high heels completed her outfit. I never asked where she got it, but I've often wondered.

Val Sultz, with all the resources of the store, copied her get-up from a picture of Little Bo Peep found in *The Mother Goose Nursery Rhymes* book. Ruffled pantaloons and all. She wore the most charming bonnet and carried a soft, toy lamb.

I, with my plain face and chubby frame, was a challenge. But the ladies met it admirably. They created a toga with a white sheet and safety pins. Then they crammed bracelets on my arms, put a wreath of leaves and flowers on my head and declared me to be a Greek goddess. That really stretched the imagination, but they didn't have a lot to work with.

Of course we all gussied up, painting our lips and cheeks with cosmetics. In the end, we made quite a foxy showing.

Granny Annie had taught Olav to make dandelion wine several years before, and the marshal still had a stash of it in his root cellar. That took care of the liquid refreshment. Annie made a big batch of pizzas, and everyone else brought potluck. So there was more than enough to eat and drink for all.

When Mr. Nielson arrived at Annie's front yard, he was dumbfounded to be met by many of the men friends he'd made while courting Granny Annie. They escorted him into her cabin where the "Muckluck fancy gals," food and wine awaited.

To say he was speechless is an understatement. When he saw his betrothed decked out as a saloon girl, I thought for a minute that he was going to have heart failure. But he quickly gathered his wits and joined in the fun. I think he thoroughly enjoyed his bachelor party.

I must say, it was one of the best shindigs ever held in Muckluck. Even more fun than a shivaree.

As Annie and Mr. Nielson grew older, their love kept blossoming. They behaved like teenagers. They may not have had many years together, but they made the most of them. Toward the end of their lives, I saw them at a school gathering. Annie sat beside his wheelchair, and they were holding hands.

Through The Eyes Of Love

She drew me away from the party.
We stood alone at the side.
"There he is," she whispered slyly
Her eyes shining brightly with pride.

"That's my husband — the one with the smile.
Even sitting you can tell that he's tall.
And isn't he handsome and charming?
He's always the beau of the ball!

His eyes are what first drew me to him.
They're shades of cerulean blue.
When he flashes them in my direction
My knees shake and turn into goo.

Just look at his long, slender fingers;
His hands molded, tender yet strong.
At his touch I am shaken and breathless.
His voice is a beautiful song."

I looked where she coyly was pointing
Saw not the Adonis she saw.
I saw an old man in a wheelchair
I saw every wrinkle, each flaw.

He was shrunken and bent and disabled,
His eyes blurred and rheumy with sap.
His hands, covered thickly with blotches
Pecked at the robe on his lap.

His voice, when he spoke, was a whisper.
It trembled and gasped with each breath.
His brow, sans the once golden ringlets
Was bald as a white skull of death.

"There he is — that's my husband!"
The man she is so smitten of
Will always be her young sweetheart
As seen through the eyes of love.

~ 13 ~

One winter, I think it was around the first of February 1946, we had more snow than we needed or wanted. It came down for nine straight days and nights, as though the angels were shaking a huge, torn, feather quilt over Alaska. Snowflakes as big as crabapples, but much softer, floated down on Muckluck. They soon covered us in snow higher than most small boys.

The big snowstorm came right before our annual Muckluck Mid-Winter Madness festival. Everyone wanted plenty of snow for the festival, but we sure thought Mother Nature was overdoing a good thing.

You know, when something unexpected and undesirable happens, you have two choices. You can sit on your fanny and bemoan your bad luck, or you can get up and do something about it. We decided to do something about it.

Every household in town had a snow shovel. So we put on our warm duds — I had just got a pair of L.L. Bean boots and was mighty proud of them — and set to shoveling paths from house to house, cabin to cabin, store to post office, school house and church.

The snow kept falling, and we kept shoveling. As we warmed to the task, the heavy duds came off. Before long, folks were in their shirt-sleeves, pants and shoepacks just shoveling away.

We scooped a long path up to the lake and cleared the snow off part of the ice. Huge piles of snow, like small mountain ranges, lined paths everywhere. And when it finally stopped snowing, we began our festival.

Anchorage had its annual Fur Rendezvous, which had begun years before when trappers brought their pelts in from the boonies to sell. But the folks in Muckluck didn't do a whole lot of trapping. Certainly not enough to celebrate.

Our festival was just to break up the monotony of winter. And to have a little fun.

We made igloos as big as chicken coops and snow chairs and animals for the kids to play on. You can't build a snow horse or dog with legs, though, 'cause they would just collapse under a kid. So our herd was, of necessity, legless.

The kids "rode" them with shouts of "giddy up" and "yippee!" The animals eventually became slick and shiny. They also turned various colors from the dyes in the kids' mittens and snowsuits. Very colorful!

And, of course, there were life-size snowmen wearing stocking caps. Some even sported the neckties men in Muckluck wouldn't wear any more. Snowwomen with impressive busts and narrow waists wore bright shawls and fancy hats. Kids flopped down in the snow and made hosts of angels all around the lake.

Hank Hazelton, an old-timer who lived near Muckluck, raised malamute sled dogs. He brought his team and sled to the party and spent the day giving rides. His dogs were gorgeous — some weighed well over a hundred pounds, and they could pull an enormous amount of weight as they ran lightly over the snow.

In case you've wondered, malamutes are not to be confused with Siberian huskies, which are slighter in build. Siberians often have blue eyes, or one blue and one brown eye. In one case I knew, each eye was divided — half blue and half brown. Siberians are pretty, too, but they're not hard workers like malamutes. Some sled dogs are part wolf. You do not want to mess with them.

But back to the festival. Men really enjoyed showing off the beards they'd been growing for weeks. Those who were particularly proud of their whiskers entered the "Best Beard" contests. We had honors for the best new and the best old beards.

If memory serves, Kenny Waldorf won in the "new" category. He really didn't have much of a beard — just some peach fuzz. But he was only a teenager, and he made such a good effort, the judges gave him the blue ribbon.

Father Sorinoff, who had been growing his beard for some forty years, had the edge in the "old" category. He won every year.

We built snow "tables" and covered them with blankets and oilcloths. Townspeople brought huge buckets of hot cocoa, piles of sandwiches and tins of cookies. We even had Granny Annie's pizzas.

Some folks skated on the lake, while others held snowshoe races and skied or tobogganed. The snow was too deep for good sledding, although some kids did sled on hard-packed paths.

Olav brought his battery-operated Zenith shortwave radio, so we had music. Sometimes it blared with big band, sometimes country and western, sometimes opera. We danced as best we could in our heavy winter footwear, tripping over our own — or our partner's — feet.

The festival lasted two days. We didn't have long to frolic, because it was winter and the days were short. But since we didn't have a lot of daylight, I think we enjoyed it all the more.

A few days after the festival, a Chinook wind blew in. The weather turned warm and the snow began to melt fast. The ground and road became mushy and dirty — give me fresh, clean snow any day.

But the folks in Muckluck, who were still giddy from the mid-winter festivities, didn't let the slush and mud get them down. Cheerfulness abounded.

Then Old Man Trouble struck. Benny Carson's beloved Sampson was found dead.

Someone spotted the dog lying on its side next to Benny's house. Blood matted the fur all over his head and had pooled in the slush under it.

Upon closer inspection, though, it was happily learned that Sampson was not dead. He was only knocked out as cold as yesterday's mashed potatoes.

Carol examined the poor critter carefully and noted a hole about the size of a pea right smack on top of the dog's head. And you know how scalp wounds can bleed.

Carol got her medical bag. and using her keen nursing skills, soon had Sampson shaved, disinfected, stitched and bandaged. During the process, he came 'round and seemed none the worse for wear. Although he did look somewhat confused and a little sheepish.

We couldn't figure out how Sampson had been injured. There wasn't a soul in town who didn't love the old fella, and there was no weapon we could think of that would cause such an injury.

It took a while, but Olav finally solved the case when he saw an icicle suddenly fall off Benny's eaves and nearly bean one of the Waldorf kids.

Of course! Sampson must have been sitting under the overhanging eave when a melting icicle fell and made a direct hit on top of his head. Then the warming temperature, along with the heat from Sampson's body, melted the icicle and left only a puddle of bloody slush.

The almost perfect "crime" was solved. And let it be a lesson to us all. Never stand under icicles — especially during a warming spell.

Snowflakes

Did you ever hold your face up
To watch the falling snow
That glitters in the moonlight
Of winter's silvery glow?

Did you notice how each snowflake
Has its own delightful form;
How each is shaped uniquely
As it dances in the storm?

For not one is like another.
God and nature see that each
Flake of snow is different
And has a lesson it can teach.

For just as every snowflake
Is unique in its design
So each of us is special
And each of us can shine.

Then as we face the storms of life
And the wintry gales of chance,
So each of us like snowflakes
Can choose to twirl and dance.

We too can let our beauty shine
Like snowflakes as they drift
Upon the troubles of the earth.
Uniqueness is our gift.

But snowflakes are so very cold
As they fall from high above,
While we can share with all our hearts
The glowing warmth of love.

~ 14 ~

One fine spring day, just after the road had dried and was fairly decent again, a white truck arrived. Inside was a portly gentleman wearing white pants and shirt, and of all things, a crisp, white apron. The back of the truck was nearly full of cardboard boxes and large tins.

It must have been a weekend, because the kids were out of school. Thelma Ward stood out in front of the schoolhouse beating chalkboard erasers together.

The white truck stopped near her. After the chalk dust settled, the driver crawled out from behind the steering wheel — no easy task because of his girth. He approached Thelma, who dropped the erasers on the porch railing.

"Where, Madam, may I find the nearest fine dining establishment?" the man in white inquired, as he smiled broadly and bowed at the waist.

The question stumped Thelma for a minute. The nearest dining establishment she could think of was her own kitchen. But that couldn't be what he meant.

Aha, she thought, he must be looking for a restaurant.

Alas, Muckluck had no such "establishment," fine or otherwise. Thelma blushed to admit the lack, but it didn't bother the large man a bit. In fact, his smile grew brighter and broader, and he clasped Thelma's hand warmly.

"Oh, that's wonderful!" he declared, in a charming French accent. "Then you'll definitely be needing my services."

Thelma, removing her hand from his huge mitt and taking a step backward, wondered just what those services might be. She was a bit leery of this overstuffed, yet courtly stranger.

"I, Madam, am a gourmet chef," he said.

The rotund chef then proceeded to tell Thelma that he had

presided in the finest eateries from San Francisco to Seattle. He now was looking for a location to showcase his talents, where they would be needed and appreciated.

"I am prepared to build and furnish a dining facility to both please the eye and provide victuals to delight the palate of the most discriminating gourmand," he said. "I, Madam, am Chef Armand Buffet at your service. My name is spelled B-u-f-f-e-t, but it is pronounced Boofay."

Well, whoa Nelly!

That set Thelma back on her heels. She hadn't heard such fancy talk since she took English 101 in college and studied Shakespeare. But, she concluded, this man wanted to start a restaurant in Muckluck. A fancy-dancy restaurant at that.

"Oh my, I hate to discourage you, Mister Chef Buffet," she said. "But I really don't think Muckluck is ready for a restaurant."

Thelma tried to explain that the folks in Muckluck did their own cooking and didn't have a lot of extra cash to spend.

"We're simple folk with simple tastes, so perhaps you should mosey on over to Anchorage and set up shop there," Thelma suggested as kindly as possible.

If you think for a minute that her words discouraged Chef "Boofay," you'd be dead wrong. He began looking for a suitable property immediately.

He soon found an old, two-story building that once had been a store. Before long, he and some of the town's boys had remodeled the ground floor into a nice restaurant and transformed the upstairs into living quarters.

It was actually quite elegant for Muckluck, with its cream-color linoleum floors, red velveteen drapes and six tables with Formica tops.

Dave Moffid built beautiful, comfortable chairs for the new restaurant, and Armand set up his stove, pots and pans in the kitchen. Chez Buffet was ready for business.

The grand opening attracted quite a crowd of curious citizens. Free coffee and cookies provided "bait."

Folks were a little reluctant to patronize Chez Buffet at first. But little by little they began to drop in to sample the chef's meals. His prices were remarkably affordable, though we were totally in the dark about some of the menu items. Whoever heard of Coq au Vin or Boeuf Bourguignonne? Over time, we learned that "Coq" was chicken and "Boeuf" was beef. Both dishes were cooked in wine.

Chef Buffet's desserts were a puzzlement, too. Sweet soufflés and tutti-frutti cake, for crying out loud.

You may find it hard to believe, but after sampling Armand's cooking, most folks soon developed a taste for the exotic and delicious.

Oh, a few old-timers held out for the more familiar moose meatloaf or grilled salmon and baked beans. And nothing beats sourdough hotcakes for breakfast.

But in time, Chef Buffet learned to mix his offerings so he always had something for everyone.

With Armand's charm, he soon had the ladies "eating out of his hand." And because he was such a non-threatening roly-poly fella, the men also came to approve of him.

Kids were crazy about him, too. He often let them taste his raw cookie dough, or lick the bowl of a soon-to-be cake. He even convinced some of them to enjoy turnips — when served with lots of margarine and brown sugar.

In time, our chef started a little cooking school. Muckluck's ladies, young and old, flocked to learn his skills and enjoy his gallantry. He was careful not to teach them anything that might some day appear on his menu, though. Those recipes were a sacred secret that kept clientele coming back for more. Chef Buffet knew what he was doing, and his restaurant became famous throughout the Kenai Peninsula.

Olav once asked me if I knew where the chef got his start-up money. I had no idea. Chef Buffet never said and, of course, we never asked.

Let me rummage around a minute. I may have one of his recipes here somewhere. Ahh, here is one I coaxed out of him. If you feel brave, you may want to try it:

Boeuf Bourguignonne

Ingredients:
1/2-pound thinly sliced salt pork
12 small onions
2 pounds lean stewing beef
1-1/2 tablespoons flour
1 teaspoon salt
4 peppercorns
1/2 bay leaf
1 or 2 cloves finely chopped garlic
1/2 teaspoon thyme or sweet marjoram

Directions:
Marinate the meat in dry, red wine overnight. Drain and reserve wine. Place meat in oven-proof dish with salt, peppercorns, bayleaf and garlic.

Cover the meat with the wine and water — 3/4 wine to 1/4 water — and bring to boil. Simmer, covered, in 300-degree oven for 2 hours.

Place pork and onions on top of the meat. Continue simmering covered for another hour, or until beef is tender. Toward the end, you can add sautéed mushrooms and chopped parsley.

Before serving with cooked noodles or mashed potatoes, pour 1/4 cup of warm brandy on the meat and touch a match to it.

Stand back — Remember what happened at my birthday party!

~ 15 ~

With the success of Chez Buffet, swarms of visitors began appearing in Muckluck. Most of them were friendly and polite, so we welcomed them and kinda enjoyed the popularity.

During the summer, folks arrived from Anchorage, Moose Pass, Hope and Seward. Some just came to "dine." Others took time to meander through town, stopping to visit with Muckluckers or dip a line in Moose Run.

Some of the locals provided music outside the restaurant on weekends, so those waiting for tables had live entertainment. Sing-alongs were encouraged, too. The musicians were happy to accept tips, so it was a win-win situation.

Then a few high school girls began gathering wild flowers on Friday afternoons and sold them to the out-of-towners. Little kids started renting fishing gear and peddling fresh salmon eggs and worms for bait.

Muckluck was becoming a town of entrepreneurs, though we didn't even know the word at the time. But along with our newfound "fame" came a small problem.

A few young bucks from Seward decided to come over to Muckluck on weekend nights and joyride around town. They would roar up and down our main street, whooping and hollering and honking their horn.

These kids had a pretty decent car, too, as the father of one of the boys was head honcho of the longshoremen. Usually five or six troublemakers would pile into his car and head for Muckluck. For several weekends we put up with the racket, and the frayed nerves they caused, to say nothing of the lack of sleep.

Then Bob Dodson, one of the road crew, had an idea. He fired up the grader one weekday afternoon and chugged down main street, raising and lowering the blade every ten feet or so. The result was a series of impressive bumps and ruts.

When the Seward roughnecks came screaming into town the next weekend, they hit those bumps and darn near shook their teeth loose. We later learned they broke a couple shock absorbers and springs and had to replace a tire with the spare. And I don't imagine they did the axle any good, either. They limped back to Seward and never bothered us like that again.

We returned to enjoying our celebrity. And it wasn't long before Chef Buffet needed help in his restaurant.

He first tried hiring some of the young locals. But they weren't inclined to work indoors handling food or dealing with the sensitivities of the chef when he went on a tangent. The younger crowd wanted to take advantage of the warm summer weather and not be cooped up inside.

So Armand advertised in the Anchorage newspaper for "experienced service providers." The first several applicants proved totally unsuitable. And the next batch wasn't any better. The chef was about to give up when two young ladies appeared at his door. They seemed to fill the bill for the upcoming summer rush.

Patsy was a blue-eyed blond. She had legs that were attractive and quick to run and fill orders. Judy, with long, black hair tied in a swinging ponytail, had curves like the old Seward Road.

Chef Buffet hired the girls on the spot. He paid them a decent wage, which was supplemented with generous tips.

They took to their task of waiting on his customers with high spirits and winning smiles. They also calmed Armand when he grew temperamental.

The gals found a cabin to live in at the edge of the woods. They made a few trips to Anchorage in a pickup to haul back necessary furniture to make their lives comfortable. Then they settled in to serve both Muckluckers and visitors.

Soon Chez Buffet was hopping with hungry customers. The chef added some new items to the menu, and everybody was happy. For a while, that is.

Then it became noticeable that nearly all the customers frequenting the restaurant were men or high school boys. Women had stopped patronizing Chez Buffet.

Maybe there was a bit of jealousy due to the pretty, new waitresses. But the men and boys packed the place from morning 'till closing time. Then they helped Patsy and Judy tidy up and escorted them home to their little nest in the woods. After all, there were wild animals around Muckluck, you know.

One day I noticed the path to the girls' cabin was deeper and wider than before. It didn't seem to me that the girls themselves would account for the expanded pathway. It looked unusually well-traveled.

So when Olav asked me if I smelled anything "funny" going on, I had to admit that I thought something was rotten in Muckluck.

The marshal decided to go undercover. With help from Carol and me, he transformed himself into a dark-haired, bearded sourdough with glasses and a limp. I wouldn't have recognized him myself.

Olav ate dinner at Chez Buffet that evening. Afterward, he insisted on helping clean the floors and tables, fill the salt and pepper shakers and put paper napkins in their holders. Another fella, one of the sawmill workers, hung around and lent a hand, too.

When everything was spic and span, the girls headed for the door.

"Well, let's go have some fun, gentlemen," Judy said.

She led the way along the deeply rutted path to the little cabin in the woods. Olav told me later he was nervous as a cat.

But when Patsy quickly shed her uniform and prompted, "You pay up front, boys!" he knew for sure what was going on. Olav was not the brightest bulb in the chandelier, but he wasn't stupid, either.

He told the girls they would have to leave Muckluck the next day, or he would take them to Seward on the charge of prostitution.

Judy and Patsy knew the jig was up. They packed their belongings that night and headed for points unknown at dawn's early light.

Chef Buffet was devastated at their abrupt abandonment. And so were a lot of guys.

But they survived, and life returned to normal on the banks of Moose Run. Armand eventually trained and hired two mature local ladies, who found they enjoyed the fellowship with the customers. They turned out to be very good waitresses and kitchen assistants.

One was a widow. The other's husband had disappeared a few years earlier, leaving her with four kids to support. The women were happy for the wages and tips.

The fairer sex began to patronize the restaurant again, and the men kept coming back for the excellent food. So it turns out that our little experience on the wild side wasn't so bad after all. Some of us wondered why the girls came to our little berg instead of staying in a bigger place like Anchorage. But they never said — and we didn't ask.

Moose Meat Stew

First you kill a moose, skin him, butcher him and save those good scraps for stew meat. Have a small glass of brandy handy.

Go in the garden and pull some potatoes, carrots and onions. Scrub well.

Put meat in a small paper bag with a couple spoonful's of flour and shake it real good to coat the meat.

In a big, heavy pot, pour a small amount of cooking oil and brown the meat thoroughly. Pour in about three cups of hot water (cold water will splatter and blister you).

Chop up the potatoes, carrots and onions and add to the meat. Cook until veggies are almost soft. Add a big can of stewed tomatoes, a can of drained kidney beans, a can of drained corn and any other vegetables you have around.

Add salt and pepper to taste. Simmer on low heat until everything is cooked.

For some reason, this always tastes better the second and third day. Serve with fresh-baked sourdough bread and peanut butter as a side dish. Dunking is encouraged.

Now you've earned the brandy. Cheers and bottoms up!

~ 16 ~

Remember that winter with the heavy snowfall I already told you about? Well, it was especially appreciated at Christmas. I don't know how people in places like California and Florida tolerate Christmas without snow.

It doesn't seem natural to me. I mean, maybe baby Jesus was born in a warm climate with palm trees and sand, but for my money, you gotta have snow for the holidays.

Christmas came before Muckluck's Mid-Winter Madness that year. But only by a month. So we were more than ready for some excitement and merriment to brighten the long, dark days.

We didn't have a lot of store-bought frills that are available nowadays. We had to make our own decorations.

Kids made miles of colored-paper chains, and we strung cranberries and popcorn until our fingers were sore. We also used tin snips to cut circles and stars out of tin cans.

Folks hoarded scraps of tinfoil from gum wrappers and cigarette packs all year. Those were used to make all kinds of Christmas ornaments. One could cut out pictures from Sears and Roebuck or "Monkey Ward" catalogs, too. And you'd be surprised how pretty we could make ordinary weeds and twigs look when we bedecked them with colorful or sparkly scraps.

Finding a decent-shaped Christmas tree to showcase our homemade ornaments, however, was a challenge. The spruce trees in our area were rather stingy of limbs and needles.

That winter, Carol and I decided we would find the perfect tree. Or die trying. We strapped on snowshoes and headed into the woods.

We hiked for a couple of hours. The two of us peered carefully at each tree we passed, rejecting each one.

Then, on the far side of a large clearing, we saw it. A tree shaped exactly like a Christmas tree is supposed to look — all fat and fluffy. It was perfect.

We were dead tired, but determined. We pushed ourselves across the meadow, until we stood before our perfect tree. Sadly, it was not one tree, but three trees growing very close together like Siamese triplets.

There was no way we could haul three trees all the way back to Muckluck. Disappointed, we turned around and trudged home. Treeless.

The next day, we set out again. But we had no better luck. As determined as we were, we finally had to admit that we were not going to find the perfect tree.

So we decided to make the most of what we had. We cut down a fairly decent tree and dragged it through the snow back to town.

By the time we got to Carol's place, we'd convinced ourselves that our tree wasn't half bad. And once we had it nailed to some crossed boards, it looked rather regal. Well, maybe not regal — but do-able. We told ourselves it would be gorgeous once we got it all decked out. And it really did turn out quite lovely.

But Dave Moffid did us one better.

Of course, being a woodcarver, he had more tools to work with. He got real creative. Dave took an old broomstick, bore holes in it and glued spruce boughs into the holes. It didn't really look like the perfect Christmas tree, but it certainly took the cake for most original.

Dave also treated the town to a figurine for its Nativity scene. Each year, he created a new figure about three feet tall, beautifully carved and painted with great care.

He carved the Virgin and Christ Child the first year. Then added Joseph the second. A shepherd joined the trio the third year. And by the year with all the snow, we had another shepherd and one wise man.

Our Nativity scene was looking very spiffy. Everyone eagerly awaited the appearance of camels, sheep and a donkey in the years to come. Dave hoped he'd live long enough to finish the scene.

Father Sorinoff always built a rough shelter in front of St. Anastasia's for the Nativity scene. And school kids gathered long, dry grass to serve as hay for the manger. Oh my, it was beautiful. We were so proud of it!

When it came to Christmas cards, most of us made our own. We started early in the fall to design and make cards from plain white paper or colored construction paper. Some of the more artistic among us drew and colored pictures, or folded and cut out snowflakes for the fronts of the cards.

Others cut pictures from magazines and catalogs and pasted them on. Thelma, always the clever one, cut garments from cloth to dress the catalog children on the front of her cards, paper-doll style. Inside we penned poems, notes and greetings. I still have a couple of the real special ones I received.

Our gifts were mostly homemade, too. A bunch of us drew names so we would have to exchange only one gift. But we put a lot of thought, time and effort into those gifts.

Many knitted and crocheted items, wooden toys, original games and baked items were given. Photo albums and calendars were popular, too. We enjoyed making those gifts as much as friends enjoyed receiving them.

As a child, I remember receiving an actual store-bought baby doll from one of the bachelors. He'd carefully fashioned a piece of beaver pelt as a wig and glued it on top of the doll's bald head. Oh, how I loved rubbing the fur against my cheek.

~ 17 ~

The highlight of the holidays was our Christmas Pageant. Preparations for the extravaganza took at least a month, and when I tell you what all went on, you'll see why.

First, we had to decorate the schoolhouse. Oh my, you never saw such lavish adornment — live green boughs, sparkly tinfoil stars, paper chains, banners and streamers galore. Benches filled the large classroom, and a modest stage was set up in front. I'll give you an example of one of our pageants. I still have the program the high school kids made.

Father Sorinoff began by reading the Christmas story from the book of Luke in the Holy Bible. He read it in English. Esther Waldorf said a prayer-blessing in her native tongue, and then the talent show began.

Carrie Smith played "Angels We Have Heard on High" on her accordiaon. Only in the program, it's misspelled as Angles.

Wendell Weeks demonstrated his prowess with the baton, while Kenny Waldorf played "Jingle Bells" on the harmonica.

Then Nell Dodson sang, in her operatic voice, a version of "Oh Holy Night" that made the hair on my neck stand up. It was that good.

Izzy Fitzheimer surprised us with his lovely rendition of "White Christmas." I honestly think he could have given Bing Crosby a run for his money. Who knew Izzy had a voice like that?

Santa also made his appearance and handed out candy and oranges to the kidlets.

Then it was time for the main event.

A three-bedspread curtain had been pulled across the front of the stage, hiding preparations for the *live* Nativity scene. The audience waited in excited anticipation for the spectacle to unfold. At last, the curtains parted.

Violet Carson was as pretty a Madonna as you've ever seen. She wore a pale-blue robe and headdress made by Molly Parkins. She smiled sweetly as she tenderly cradled her month-old baby daughter in her arms. The child was so swaddled that nobody could tell she wasn't a boy. Violet's husband, Benny, stood proudly behind Mother and Child, holding a small, dim lantern, doing his best Joseph impersonation.

The day before the pageant, Olav was coaxed into visiting Mrs. Eversall to ask for the loan of her cow and goat. Olav could be a charmer when he set his mind to it. After much persuasion, Mrs. E reluctantly agreed to the loan if Olav would take personal responsibility for her animals' safety. And she wanted a front-row seat at the pageant so she could keep an eye on her property.

Behind the Holy Family were piles of brush and branches, and among the foliage stood old Bossy and the goat. Esther had cleverly fashioned a hump and cinched it onto the cow to give her the appearance of a camel. In the semi-darkness, it could have fooled those of us sitting toward the rear of the room.

The goat, which was supposed to be a sheep, stuck his head around the brush and chomped away at anything within reach, including Joseph's robe. A few chickens pecked at cornmeal scattered on the stage.

The audience gaped in awe at the beautiful, heart-warming tableau. But seconds after the curtain was pulled open, the cow let out a bellow like a foghorn.

The sudden racket scared the goat, which leaped over the pile of greenery, scattering squawking chickens right and left. She then raced down the aisle toward the door. The ensuing fiasco woke "Baby Jesus," who began to scream at the top of her lungs.

Amid the chaos, each person lit a small candle and held it high as we sang, "Silent night, holy night, all is calm, all is bright" for the grand finale.

Then with many a cheery "Merry Christmas!" and warm hugs all 'round, we tugged on our heavy coats, caps and mittens and made our way home under a night sky aglow with stars.

Topping the evening off in all its glory, the Northern Lights whipped and flashed multi-colored ribbons of splendor across the dome of the heavens, whispering secrets of the universe. And above and beyond it all, I swear you could hear echoes of the Bethlehem angels' song.

An hour later, all was calm and all was bright that Holy Christmas Eve in Muckluck.

Mike

His halo is crooked, his wings are a sight,
His gown is all tattered and torn.
His bare little feet are just covered with grime
And his harp is not played – it's just worn.

His snubbed, freckled nose wrinkles up in a grin
And his mouth is a little too wide
For there's something a'missing right there in the front:
Two teeth, if you just peek inside.

He looks like a typical fella all right
Who's been playing a tough game of ball.
That's what he's been doing behind the pearl gates:
A double, a triple, A HOME RUN!" and all.

But now he's been summoned to come to The Hall
Where The King sits up high on His throne.
How he wished he had known he'd be called there today.
How he wished, oh, he wished he had known.

But when Gabriel came and said, "Get ready, Mike,
You've been summoned to come to The Hall."
There hadn't been time to clean up and to change
Just hadn't been time, that was all.

He'd wiped off his hands on the hem of his gown
And got rid of some limp bubblegum
But other than that, why he looked just a fright.
Oh, why had God asked him to come?

Why couldn't it wait 'til he spit-shined his harp
And slipped sandals upon his brown toes?
But God just can't wait for excuses like that
He's busy — that everyone knows.

So now at the door of the Great Hall he stands
Our hero, with one crooked wing
And waits for the trumpets to bellow their call
Announcing small Mike to The King.

At last all the silence of Heaven is rent
By the trumpeters' call, clear and loud.
Poor Mike's shattered nerves react with a jolt
And Mike jumps a foot off the cloud.

The great doors are opened, exposing a view
Of magnificent splendor so bright
Mike squinted his eyes and tried hard to see,
But he couldn't — so brilliant the light.

His heart pounded madly against his small ribs
As one step, then another he took.
Only when he was finally right up to the throne
Would he venture another small look.

For never in all of Mike's ten thousand years
(Which in our time is counted just seven)
Had Mike ever seen such a wonderful face:
"The face that illuminates Heaven."

Ah, but tongue cannot tell and pen cannot write
Enough words to imagine the thrill
Of a small, dusty cherub who kneels facing God
While eternity stops and stands still.

But then the great King, stepping down from His throne
Placed his own gentle hand on Mike's head.
"Now Michael," he said, "I have great need of you.
You've a big job ahead, son," He said.

He went on to say in that wonderful voice
How he hoped Mike was up to the test
By doing his duty, fulfilling God's trust,
And Mike said he'd give it his best.

And so Mike was happy as leaving The Hall
He prepared for his journey to Earth.
He arrived here on time to start his first job
At exactly the hour of Christ's birth.

On that very night, the most holy of nights,
When the stars in the sky blazed their fire
Archangels and cherubim sang forth their joy.
And Mike? Why he led the choir!

~ 18 ~

As long as I'm thinking about Christmas, I have another memory I'd like to share with you. It involves Mrs. Eversall - minus the cow.

I was rummaging through the woods looking for branches or dried berries to use as decorations for my cabin. Before I knew it, I found myself at Mrs. Eversall's homestead. As I got closer, I was amazed to see bright objects all over the front of her cabin.

Since Mrs. Eversall had long since forgiven Carol and me for zapping Bossy, I dared approach the place for a closer look. Why, there were hundreds of stars, circles, squares and diamond shapes cut from tin cans individually nailed to the logs with tiny nails. They sparkled and shone like gems in the early afternoon sunlight.

I was charmed! So I went up to her door and knocked softly. Soon Mrs. E appeared.

You know, she wasn't nearly as mean as we had thought. I think she was just out of the habit of dealing with people, living alone for so long. People can get that way, ya know. She invited me to come in and sit a spell.

I asked her about the tin decorations while we munched on some moose jerky. She seemed to want to talk about them, so I sat quietly while she told her story.

Mrs. Eversall said that back around 1918, she and her husband were living in Vancouver, Washington. Mr. Eversall had been a carpenter and did very well for himself. They owned a little farm with a cow, a pig and a few chickens.

Mrs. Eversall took great pride in their home. She was proud of their only child, too. They'd named him Georgie, after his father. With World War I winding down, life was good for the Eversalls.

Then that terrible flu epidemic hit. Soldiers coming home from Europe carried that sickness and it spread like wildfire. Thousands of people in America died. Little Georgie was only eight years old when he got sick.

Despite all her motherly care and doctors' remedies, Georgie died just before Christmas. He was buried on Christmas Eve. Heartbroken, Christmas would never be the same for the Eversalls.

As the new year arrived, Mr. Eversall became more and more despondent. He couldn't be consoled, though his wife tried her best to bring him some peace, if not joy. She hurt awful, too, but her faith and courage got her through that bleak and terrible time.

On February 3, at dinner time, Mrs. Eversall waited for her husband to come home from a job he was working on. She'd fixed his favorite chicken and dumplings, hoping that would please him. When he hadn't arrived by eight o'clock, she became very worried.

Although she was alarmed, she still had chores to do. So she went out to check on the animals in the barn. And that's where she found George Eversall. He had hanged himself from the rafters.

Now I've got to tell you, Mrs. Eversall's eyes were dry while she related that horrible experience to me. I wasn't as brave — I had to wipe tears from my eyes as she continued her tale.

Mrs. Eversall told me that she just couldn't stay in Vancouver any more. A friend of hers was moving to Alaska, and she decided to go along. She sold her beautiful home and the livestock and caught the *North Star* at Seattle. How she hated to leave her mister and Georgie behind, she said.

When they arrived in Seward, her friend got a job as a bookkeeper at the steamship company office. Mrs. Eversall couldn't find work, so she moved on to Hope, where she hired a couple young fellows to help her build her cabin deep in the woods.

She bought Bossy from a fellow named Logan, and he threw in the goat for free. She named the goat Uncle Sam, because she thought he looked like those recruitment posters of America's Uncle Sam pointing his finger, saying "Uncle Sam Wants YOU!"

I think it was the beard that made the resemblance.

Mrs. Eversall said she was pretty lonely in her little cabin that first Christmas. She hadn't yet made any friends in Hope or

Muckluck. But she wanted to recognize the birth of our Lord. She didn't have any decorations, but she did have tin snips and a lot of tin cans. She cut the tops and bottoms off the cans, made them into various shapes and nailed them to the front of the cabin.

"Every year I take them down on New Year's Day and put them in boxes to use the next year," Mrs. Eversall said. "And each year I add more. I do it in memory of my husband and little Georgie."

Well, that sad story really got to me. I decided to do something special for Mrs. Eversall.

I got a bunch of folks together just before Christmas, and armed with flashlights and lanterns, we made our way through the dark to her cabin. We then shined our lights on those tin decorations. They looked just plain beautiful. Can you imagine hundreds of cut-outs glowing in the darkness? And a big, fat candle flickered in the front window to complete the picture.

Then, as planned, we began to sing. After the first song, the door opened. There stood Mrs. Eversall, dressed warmly in a man's greatcoat with a wool scarf around her white hair and fur mukluks on her feet.

For a moment she just stood there amidst all the shining tin ornaments, her eyes as bright as any of them. And then she began to clap her mittened hands.

When we started the next song, she joined in. We sang every Christmas song we could think of, and she sang with us all the way to the end of our "program."

When we finished, Mrs. Eversall invited us into her cabin. It was crowded, but we didn't mind a whit. We'd come prepared with all sorts of baked goodies. Mrs. Eversall provided coffee.

She didn't have enough cups to go around. But she had lots of clean tin cans saved up for her next ornament snipping project. We were just as happy drinking from those tin cans as from the finest bone china. Muckluckers took their coffee when, where and however they could get it.

And the pure joy on Mrs. Eversall's face is one of my fondest Christmas memories.

~ 19 ~

I already told you about Mr. Snyder, the old fella who had trouble with Carol's enema. But there are things you don't know about him yet. He was a corker, all right.

Mr. Snyder came to Alaska many years before I knew him. Back when he was much younger, and Muckluck was not even a real town. He came, like so many others, with a thirst for gold — and like most everybody else, he mucked with no luck. But for some reason he stayed.

He built himself a cabin up the creek a mile or so and kept to himself. His only companion was a big, white husky named Redoubt, after the majestic mountain over across Cook Inlet.

He hunted and trapped — and occasionally dipped a pan in the creek in hopes of capturing a nugget or two. He planted a garden every spring, and like the rest of us, he lived off the land.

He must of liked his own cooking, too, for I never saw him in Chez Buffet. Mr. Snyder didn't go to the post office, either, because he never received or sent any mail.

Once I saw him at Sultz's store buying ammo, canned milk and salt. He returned my greeting with a polite nod and a "Howdy, Ma'am," but that's all I got out of him.

Olav was probably the only person Mr. Snyder ever touched bases with — not counting the enema experience he had with Carol. The marshal told me he'd been out to the Snyder place several times to check on the old man.

He learned a little about Mr. Snyder over the years, which I'll pass on as a sort of warm-up for what happened later. For one thing, Olav learned Mr. Snyder had a first name. Solomon.

One can only hope as a child he was called Sol. He didn't say, and Olav didn't ask. But when his tongue loosened after many cups of tar-black coffee, Solomon Snyder opened up a little.

He offered Olav small tidbits of information during each visit. For instance, Solomon was born in Saskatoon, Saskatchewan, Canada, in 1863, while the Civil War raged in the United States. He married a young Native woman named Nella, and they had a child. Both of them were killed in a tragic boating accident.

Besides an uncle about his own age, Solomon had no other known relatives. When gold was discovered in the Yukon in 1896, Solomon and his Uncle Zeb, figuring they had nothing to lose and much to gain, joined the hopeful mob in Skagway. Solomon said he heard over 100,000 people had the same idea.

"Skagway was a hell-hole," was how he described that wretched place.

The night before they were to start their climb over the Chilkoot Trail and Pass, Uncle Zeb got into a fight with one of Soapy Smith's henchmen over a pair of Levi pants. He was brutally stabbed. Solomon was minding his own business in another part of town, and only heard by chance that the Smith gang had thrown Zeb's bloody corpse into the icy waters of Lynn Canal. And that was that. Solomon was truly alone.

Mr. Snyder didn't like to talk about the terrible trek over the Pass, nor about the trials encountered once he reached the Yukon Territory. He found no gold, so he made his way to Nome when the Rush moved there. Still no luck.

For years he wandered around Alaska, trying his hand at this and that. He never found a woman to love, a golden treasure or a place of peace and security — until he discovered Muckluck.

He was reluctant to give details in his visits with Olav, but he managed a smile when he said Muckluck came into his life while he was hiking from Moose Pass to Hope one day.

While he walked through the community that day, he noticed that people nodded, but nobody spoke other than to say "Howdy!" He liked that. So he built his little cabin out in the woods and acquired a series of dogs, the latest and best being Redoubt.

He tried raising mink, too. He had a nice little family of the critters just about ready to donate their coats to the furrier in

Anchorage, when a pack of wolves discovered them. Solomon and Redoubt were off fishing and never knew a thing until they returned home and saw the carnage. He didn't have the heart to start over after that.

And that's all we knew about Mr. Snyder. Actually, Olav told me in strict confidence, and I never told a living soul until now. We figured Mr. Snyder had found his peaceful place. Not too many people ever do, you know, so we were happy to just leave him alone.

Then one day a man drove into town in a snazzy new Ford. Mr. Carmichael was his name. He stopped at Chez Buffet for a bite of lunch and started asking questions about a man named Sam Solomon. No one at the restaurant had heard of such a man.

He next went to the post office and inquired of Molly. But she had never heard of Sam Solomon.

The stranger finally located Olav, who figured he knew Sam Solomon but kept his trap shut until he heard the whole story.

Mr. Carmichael told Olav he was a private investigator, hired by the First National Bank of Seattle to locate this Mr. Solomon. Turns out that "Solomon Snyder" was an alias.

Olav had a sinking feeling that maybe his friend Sol was wanted for bank robbery — or worse. So he kept mum while Mr. Carmichael went on with his story.

He said that when Solomon and his Uncle Zeb were in Skagway, there had been a fight during which Zeb was knifed and thought dead. But one of the saloon gals claimed his nearly dead body and nursed him back to health. The nephew, hearing falsely that his uncle had been killed and was at the bottom of the Lynn Canal, moved on.

Following Zeb's lengthy and painful recovery, he started searching for Sol. The uncle made his way to the Yukon, but Sol was long gone.

Zeb, lucky dog that he was, may not have found his nephew, but he did find a fortune in gold. He was one of the very few to hit pay dirt, and he wisely returned to Seattle with it intact.

He'd learned his lesson in Skagway. Zeb invested his money in the First National Bank of Seattle, where it had been collecting interest ever since.

Zeb lived frugally and alone. When he passed to his reward, they found a will in his boarding-house room that left his fortune to his nephew — one Sam Solomon.

Olav was floored. He took Mr. Carmichael out to Solomon's cabin. The private eye repeated the tale to a dumbfounded, but now filthy rich, Solomon Snyder, aka Sam Solomon, and his trusty dog, Redoubt.

You may wonder what Mr. Snyder did with his new-found wealth. Well, he sure didn't spend any of it. He said he already had everything a man could ask for.

Instead, he set up a trust fund at the First National Bank of Seattle that would provide funds for every child who graduated from high school in Muckluck to attend the college or university of his or her choice. And if ever there weren't any more kids graduating from Muckluck, the remainder of the trust would go to the University of Alaska to be used as college grants to needy Alaska-born children.

And that's the end of that story.

~ 20 ~

I recollect the day little Robby Dodson came tearing into the schoolhouse with really big news. He was in such a lather he could hardly talk. But Miss Ward calmed him down by rubbing his back and giving him gulps of water from the dipper in the tin bucket.

I was visiting the school that day, helping a couple kids who were having trouble with their arithmetic. I saw Robby's little face as white as paper, except for big, red blotches on his cheeks from running. He was shaking to beat the band, near to sobbing, and taking big gulps of air as snot ran from his nose. His eyes were big as baseballs.

When he was finally able to talk, he said he'd been down by the creek, throwing rocks at an old log on the other side. The rocks kept falling short, so he determined to stay at it until he finally hit the mark.

Boys will do things like that, you know, and that's why they're so often late for school or church. But they're never late for dinner or other eats. Early on, boys develop a stubborn streak that often stays with them the rest of their lives. Sometimes that's a good thing — but usually not. It's just a fact of life.

My goodness, I can wander off, can't I! Let's get back to the story.

Robby said he bent down to pick up another rock. When he straightened up, he saw a woman coming toward him. She was carrying a big basket, overflowing with clothes. As she came closer, Robby could see that she wore a long, dark dress, mostly covered with a gray apron.

"Her hair was kinda messed up, but pulled back away from her face," Robby said. "She wasn't real old like Granny Annie, but not as young as Violet, either."

Which left quite a gap to choose from, I must say. Robby said she looked tired or worried, or maybe sad, as she came slowly along the creek bank toward him.

The really scary thing was that she didn't seem to actually walk. She just sorta floated about a foot off the ground. She didn't acknowledge Robby in any way. Although she looked straight ahead, she seemed to look right through him.

Now young Robby had lived in Muckluck all his life, and he knew every single soul in town. And they knew him. But he swore he'd never seen this lady before or anybody who looked like her.

"She looked like she was made of glass or smoke, not skin and bones," he said.

As Robby watched, mouth agape and knees trembling, the lady put down the basket and began taking clothes out. She then put them into the shallow part of the creek where the kids liked to wade and play.

"And then" Robby yelled, "she just disappeared!"

By this time, the whole school was in a dither. The smaller kids cried, and the big ones shook their heads and mumbled to each other. One girl tried to hide under her desk. Another yelled for her mama. Everybody had the heebie-jeebies.

Poor Thelma had a beast of a time restoring order. When the kids finally calmed down, she dismissed the class for the day and told them to go straight home. Which you may be sure they did, as fast as their little legs could carry them.

Thelma came over to my place and we talked about Robby's strange story. She was more than a little shaky, and I'll admit, I had the creeps myself. We decided to go talk to Olav and see what he thought about it.

Not much, it turned out. After he heard the story, he just scoffed and said that little boys tend to make up stories and that was obviously what Robby had done.

Thelma did not agree. She stuck by her guns and insisted that if Olav had seen that child he would have believed him. I tried to be neutral.

The three of us chewed on it for a while, without reaching any conclusions. We finally agreed to leave well enough alone, wait, and see what happened.

What happened was that a bunch of parents came to the school later that day to get Thelma's "take" on the story. She told them that as strange and unbelievable as it seemed, she believed Robby had seen what he said.

Robby's mother chimed in that her boy had never told a lie in his life. And several of the other parents believed her. A few of the men snickered at the idea of a ghost, and Robby's father came close to punching one Doubting Thomas on the nose.

Thelma sent for Olav, who ran into me on the way to the school. We arrived to find the crowd pretty evenly divided on the subject of ghosts. Olav let them ramble on for a while and then called for order.

"Since nobody here can prove one way or t'other, I ask you to go home and forget the whole durn thing," he told the crowd. "I would remind you that you are Muckluckers, and Muckluckers do not fight about things like, well, like ghosts."

With heads low in embarrassment, and amid much grumbling and mumbling, the group broke up and returned to their homes. After a few days, even the kids stopped talking about it. Robby's ghost soon was forgotten.

Until a year or so later, that is, when Orvill Nivens came tearing into Chez Buffet and reported that he'd just seen a woman washing clothes in Moose Run. That got everyone's attention.

It's true, we didn't have electric washing machines, but by then most of us had private generator-powered washers. Nobody washed clothes in the creek, that's for darn sure.

We all wanted to hear details. But shy Orvill was reluctant to admit that after gaping at this strange apparition for several seconds, she suddenly disappeared.

Orvill said he walked over to the creek and looked for soapsuds in the water, but it was clear as crystal. There was neither hide nor hair of the lady.

Some of us hot-footed on over to Moose Run to look for ourselves. But we found all as it should be. No suds, no clothes, no lady.

Orville's experience got everyone thinking about Robby's "ghost sighting." Then the subject of hauntings was the buzz around town again for a few weeks. Some thought Orvill was pulling a prank, but others, especially those of us who saw him at Chez Buffet that day, believed he was telling the truth.

As spring started popping out in full bloom, though, other matters began occupying our minds and time. Gardens were planted, homes battered by winter's icy blasts were repaired, cold weather clothes were stored away and summer duds aired out for the expected warm weather.

People who think Alaska is always ice, snow and cold just don't know how beautiful summers usually are on the Kenai. I say "usually," because once in a while we got a stinker with lots of rain. But that's rare. We *so* enjoyed and appreciated our glorious summers.

Carol and I decided it was time to go fiddlehead fern hunting. If you don't know about fiddlehead ferns, I'm going to enlighten you here and now. A fiddlehead fern is actually the new tip of an Ostrich fern frond. But hardly anybody knows them by that name.

They're beautiful, lush, green ferns that grow in shaded, moist places. Some grow as tall as your waist and as big around as four feet or so. In early spring, they each bring forth seven tightly curled "baby" fronds that look like the yellow-brown-green snail shells children draw. Left alone, these babies will unfurl into full, feathery fronds. You must not pick more than three off any fern, or the next year you'll find a dead fern in your favorite hunting spot.

When you get your fiddlehead babies home, you wash them, peel off the part that looks like a peanut casing, and then boil up a batch in water. You boil 'em once, and then drain the water. You put in fresh water and boil 'em again until they're tender to a fork, but not mushy.

Then you drain them, sauté 'em in a bit of butter or margarine, and sprinkle with salt and pepper. If you follow the directions right, you'll have a scrumptious side dish for your moose steak and baked potatoes. They're reported to be rich in good stuff, and taste a little like asparagus.

So now that you know more about fiddleheads than you ever wanted to know, I'll tell you what happened the day that Carol and I went hunting. We found more than we bargained for.

We were a couple miles from town, out in the woods. Carol, as always when going afield, carried her 30.06. I carried a medium-size pail. You don't want to pick too many fiddleheads at one time, 'cause they're best eaten the same day.

As we came upon a nice patch of ferns, I stubbed my toe and nearly fell on my face. After recovering, I kicked at whatever I'd tripped over. It turned out to be a hunk of rock.

I noticed the stone was smooth and shaped. Curiosity made me stoop over for a closer look. I brushed away rotten leaves, twigs and dirt that partially hid it.

As more of the rock became visible, I realized I had stumbled over a fallen tombstone. I yelled for Carol to come and help me uncover the rest of it.

The words written on the stone were hard to read thorugh the thick dirt and years of decaying vegetation. But we brushed and dug with our fingernails and small twigs until we finally made out the writing.

Avis Harmon
Washerwoman
1903

The hairs on the back of my neck stood straight up. I'll wager Carol's did the same. We stared at the stone, then at each other. Cautiously we peered into the dim forest, afraid of what we might see.

I'd like to say we saw the washerwoman's ghost that day. But we didn't. We high-tailed it back to town and forgot all about our fiddlehead ferns. We talked about Avis the whole way back.

Who was she? How did she die? Why was she buried way out there so far from town? Did anybody miss her? Somebody must have cared about her to put a stone marker on her grave.

We didn't know how to handle our "find." So we did what Muckluckers usually did. We went to see Olav.

Over a mug of steaming coffee, Olav listened to our story. He pursed his lips and scratched his head and grunted a few times as we rambled on. What to do? What to do?

After much conversation about how our discovery might affect the folks, we decided to keep our traps shut and not tell a living soul.

Olav was afraid there could be panic. He thought someone might want to dig up the grave, even. And perhaps people would start seeing ghosts all over the place. We decided it just wouldn't serve any good purpose to get everybody in an uproar.

So we kept our mouths shut. I have never told anyone about Avis until I told you today. Oh, we'd talk about the washerwoman among ourselves, and once the three of us went out to the grave so Olav could see it for himself.

We didn't want anyone else to find the tomestone and get any crazy ideas, so we found a big rock shaped like a pyramid. The three of us lugged it over and placed it on top of the grave. That way we could find it again if we wanted to.

Sometimes Carol and I took wildflowers and placed them on the stone. Though we never saw the washerwoman, she was never far from our minds. I had my own idea about what happened to Avis and I wrote a poem about it.

Sweet Revenge

In death her body, cold and still
Lies where no one can see.
She does not feel the evening chill
Nor see the shadows flee.

The man who took her as his wife
Grew weary of her charms
And chose to sacrifice her life
For another woman's arms.

With blade of steel he pierced her heart
And watched the life blood flow.
She vowed she never would depart
And never let him go.

Now, though he wanders, free at last
He never feels alone.
She haunts his nights and holds him fast.
He hears her dying moan.

He sees her face upon the wall
And smells her putrid breath.
A glimpse of shadow in the hall,
She's with him still, in death.

His soul is eaten up with guilt;
His mind is wracked with pain.
He's grieving for the blood he spilt.
It's driving him insane.

The torture never goes away.
He's haunted by his wife.
Until at last there comes the day
The coward takes his life.

Still she doth walk along the paths
She knew so well in life.
And grieves for love that might have been
When she was Henry's wife.

~ 21 ~

It may seem to you like there was always some kind of mystery going on in Muckluck. But you know, I'm talking about a twenty year period. For the most part, things were pretty quiet in our little town.

Life went on. Babies were born, people died, newcomers settled in and some moved on to other pastures. So I'm just hitting the high spots. And sometimes, I'll admit, I get these happenings out of order.

But that doesn't matter. What matters is that these things happened. Maybe some day you'll write down my stories. Like the one I'm going to tell you now.

One fine morning around 1947, give or take a year or so, a young man walked into town and sat down on the steps of Sultz's store. He looked to be just out of his teens, with sandy blond hair and just a hint of a beard. His eyes were deep gray. They looked like they'd witnessed things that made him very sad. His clothes were well worn, but fairly clean.

He pulled a pocket knife from his duffle bag and picked up a willow branch. He then began to whittle as he sat on the step.

Some of the town kids spotted him before long and sidled over to make his acquaintance. They gave their names and asked his.

"Willy," was all he said. When they asked where he came from, he said, "Oh, here and there."

The kids had not yet mastered the Muckluckers' unwritten rule. If they don't tell, you don't ask. So they kept asking.

Whenever they got the chance, they questioned him about his past. But Willy didn't tell 'em anything about his life before Muckluck. He did, however, spin yarns to entertain them.

Every day after school, and during that summer vacation, kids would find Willy and beg for a story. So as Willy whittled willow whistles to give the children, he'd make up the most entertaining tales. Sometimes they were about animals that thought they were people and acted and talked accordingly. Other times they featured giants or elves or dinosaurs.

Whatever the subject, Willy always came through with a good story. Sometimes he also made up games and played right along with the children. The kids just loved him. The parents were fond of him, too, as he kept their kids entertained and out of mischief.

If a parent needed a babysitter, they asked Willy. He was always obliging and never charged for the privilege. Lucky was the child who Willy tended, for he or she always got a private story, all their very own.

I remember a small, vivacious Mucklucker sharing a "once upon a time" story that Willy had told her. Seems a little girl named Jane lived in the deep forest. She had eyes as blue as forget-me-nots and hair as gold as the sunshine shimmering on yonder lake. She was a happy little girl because she had fine animal friends.

One, a large, Kodiak brown bear named Fuzzy, was Jane's protector. She always felt safe with Fuzzy nearby. Another friend was a snowshoe rabbit named Harry. He provided for Jane and always found the best berries for her to eat.

Silver was a gray wolf that howled softly at the moon and sang Jane to sleep each night. And Wesley, a weasel that magically changed his brown coat to white in the wintertime, was Jane's sleeping buddy. He'd curl up under her chin and snore softly all night long.

Jane and her friends lived in a cave beside the Kenai River. They played games like hide-and-seek, hunted for wildflowers and splashed in a shallow pond at a bend in the river. Sometimes they caught minnows, but they always let them go free again to grow into big trout like Rainbow, another friend.

And so the days passed pleasantly. Jane talked to her friends a lot, but they never talked to her. She eventually ran out of things to talk about and wished for someone who would answer her.

She longed to hear another human voice. But she only heard the wind whispering in the trees — and the roars, howls and squeaks of the animals.

One day Jane was out digging for worms to feed to Rainbow when she heard a voice. It was an honest-to-goodness human voice, and it was singing, "You are my sunshine, my only sunshine...."

Jane jumped up, washed her hands quickly and followed the sound until she came to a small clearing. There, sitting on a fallen log, was a beautiful lady.

She was singing to a man stretched out in the grass. He smiled as he listened to her lovely voice. Jane held her breath and listened, too.

When the song ended, the lady smiled sadly.

"Oh, John," she said. "I wish we had a child to share our love!"

"So do I, Laura," John told his wife.

Jane crept from her hiding place and was swept into the lady's arms. John put his arms around both of them, and they hugged and hugged. Then they asked if Jane would like to be their little girl.

Without blinking an eye, Jane yelled "YES!"

But then she remembered her animal friends, and she knew she couldn't bear to leave them. She asked if they could come, too.

"But of course they can," John and Laura said in unison. "They can live on our homestead with us for ever after."

And that's how Willy ended the story, that little girl told me. No wonder Willy was such a favorite with the kids and parents.

His stories always had happy endings. Even if they were a little scary, like on Halloween, when the kids begged for a "spook story."

Willy was with us less than a year, when he showed up at my cabin, around breakfast time. I invited him to pull up a chair and have some sourdough hotcakes with blueberry syrup. He was lucky that day, as sometimes I didn't have syrup. On those days, I made some out of brown sugar and water. It was a bit thin, but better than nothing.

Anyway, we sat and ate. Then we drank several cups of coffee before Willy looked pensively at me and finally broke the news.

"Kate, I've got to be movin' on," he said.

"Oh, no," I groaned. "We all love you, Willy. Must you go?"

"Yeah," he answered sadly, "It's time."

He then shared his story. It was the last tale he ever told in Muckluck.

"It's this way, Katie," he told me. "I was sent to Italy in 1944 and fought near Castel d'Aiano that April. It was horrible. Worse than you can even imagine."

He said he saw more fear, pain and death than anyone should see. He witnessed his best friend's head disappear in a burst of blood, flesh and bone. He heard buddies cry out for their mothers, as they tried to stop blood gushing from unsurvivable wounds.

"Six of us were crouching in a foxhole when a grenade was lobbed right at us from behind some blasted up olive trees," Willy said. "It landed at our feet, and we just stared at the damn thing, paralyzed with fear."

Then something clicked in his head. He heard his father's voice.

"Son, you just go and do what needs to be done, the voice said," Willy told me.

Willy knew what he had to do. He snatched up that grenade and threw it as hard as he could right back where it came from.

It exploded and killed three Italian soldiers. Willy saw their bodies fly through the air, and then blood and body parts rained down.

"I yelled at the other guys in my squad to run for their lives," he said. "I promised to give them cover fire."

He said he blasted away in the direction he'd thrown the grenade. When his pals were safely away in a thick stand of woods, he shot a couple more of the enemy who were headed toward them. Then he took off dodging bullets as he ran.

"I'm not proud I killed those men," Willy sighed sadly. He added that they were just people like us with families who loved them. "I hated killing then, and I hate it to this day."

His company was sent to Germany shortly after that skirmish. Two of the fellows who were with him at Castel d'Aiano were wounded there. Two more were killed. He lost track of the sixth one.

Willy took a bullet in his leg during a battle. He was dragged to a field medical unit before being sent to an Army hospital in England. He said he saw dozens of men, wounded in mind and body, struggling to stay alive in that hospital.

"It was pitiful," he said. "Almost as bad as being at the front."

After he healed from his wound, the Army sent him back to the states, where he was discharged. He said he moved in with his folks on their farm and just tried to hide.

A telegram arrived a few months later. President Truman wanted to give him the Medal of Honor.

"I didn't want it," he said. "I didn't deserve it."

Then a telephone call came from the White House. Willy and his parents were invited to the official ceremony.

"We didn't go, so the medal was sent to my folks' house."

Willy didn't want any part of the war or honors or presidents. He needed time to be alone, in peace, to find himself and learn to live with his nightmare memories.

So he boarded a ship headed for Alaska and got off in Seward. When he heard about Muckluck, he took a train to Moose Pass and hoofed it into town.

"I've found a lot of comfort here, especially with those kids," he said. "They've never learned to hate and kill — yet. But I've got to keep moving."

He said he needed to find another place to grieve and heal. But he would never forget Muckluk.

Both Willy and I had our handkerchiefs out by that time. We held hands, wiped the tears away and blew our noses.

I kissed his cheek and bade him God speed at the door. Then he told me his real name — he made me swear not to ever tell anyone else. I never did. And I'm not going to tell you now. But I looked up the names of all the Medal of Honor winners once, and sure enough, there was our Willy.

A Mother's Plea

I watched him as he walked away
So young and brave and tall;
His uniform all fresh and new
To answer Freedom's call.

He raised his hand — a brief salute,
A grin, a wave was all
My son could offer as he left
To answer Duty's call.

I stood and watched the plane depart.
My heart was cold as lead.
My son was going off to war;
My soul was filled with dread.

Recalling him in baby days:
His chubby arms outspread
The golden curls now sweat-soaked
By the helmet on his head.

I saw him once again a child
All gangly leg and arm;
Those legs now marching him into
The cruel embrace of harm.

I saw him in his teen years
Filled with joy and charm
Now bravely going off to fight,
The tyrants to disarm.

Though I can't stand beside him
And we'll be so far apart
He's always there inside me
At the center of my heart.

I ask the Father of us all
To heed my fervent plea
And keep him safe — and when war's done
To bring him home to me.

~ 22 ~

I suppose it was bound to happen sooner or later. Kids being kids, you know. They get to an age where they want to experience new things, see the world, test their wings a little. It's a rough time for the kids and for the parents.

It was springtime again, the snow had melted, pussy willows were fat and furry. Blood stirred in sluggish veins, and the kids were restless. Especially the seven kids who were graduating in June. We had four boys and three girls in the senior class that year.

Through a letter from a cousin in Wisconsin, one of them learned that it was a tradition for graduates to enjoy something called a Senior Skip. Apparently, in the states, seniors took trips to places like Washington, D.C., or San Francisco or someplace equally exciting.

Our kids didn't have much to choose from, as Seward was the only town of any size we could drive to in those days. The highway to Anchorage didn't open until 1951.

So Arnie, James, Ronald, Buzz, Helen, Esther and Rose went as a united force to plead their case for a trip to Seward to Thelma Ward. She had become principal of the school and now had four other teachers on her staff.

The kids hemmed and hawed and wasted time until Thelma told them she didn't have all day. She then asked what they wanted.

James, the son of one of the more prominent families in town, was the boldest of the group. A good-looking kid with dark, curly hair and hazel eyes, he fancied himself somewhat of a "ladies' man."

He had more advantages than most of the Muckluck kids. Because his folks had a bit of money, and since James was their only son, he was spoiled more than he deserved. He actually owned a bicycle.

James stepped forward and said they wanted to go on a Senior Skip to Seward.

"Have you talked this over with your parents?" Thelma asked.

"Oh yes, of course," James replied. "And they said it was okay with them if you say we can go."

Thelma sighed.

"All right, I'll speak with them," she said. "Then I'll let you know. In the meantime, go back to class and don't get your hopes too high."

She doubted that all the parents had been consulted, much less given their permission, but she was willing to give the benefit of the doubt. Sort of. Part of her hated to disappoint the kids, but something told her this plan had the earmarks of a real fiasco.

That evening Thelma called at all seven homes. One set of parents said they thought it would be fun for the kids. Another had never heard of the plan, but thought it would be okay, considering the graduates were good kids and deserved a break.

Other parents, especially those who had daughters, did not like the idea at first. But upon further consideration, they agreed. If other parents thought it was a good idea, they didn't want to be party-poopers.

One mother said flat out she would't let her son skip anything. When she learned the kids wouldn't be going alone, however, she went along with the idea.

So the consensus was that if they had proper chaperoning and careful supervision, the kids could go to Seward for one day and one night.

The kids were jubilant and began to plan their trip. There was much to consider, including how they would travel, who would chaperone, and how they would get money to pay for hotel rooms and eats.

The graduates themselves worked out the details. They contacted the two men in town who owned pickup trucks with homemade shells or canopies in back. One of the guys was planning a trip to Seward anyway, and the other was bribed with a couple cans of Copenhagen. They agreed to let the boys ride in the back of one pickup and the girls in the other. Transportation problem solved.

Now for the chaperones. You would not believe how busy all the adults suddenly became when asked to help watch the kids. Even Carol, who was usually up for anything, had plans that could not be changed.

Finally, Orvill Nivens, the same fella who had been unjustly suspected of being a sneak thief, agreed to keep an eye on the boys. And I, never one to think fast on my feet, couldn't come up with an excuse to refuse and agreed to chaperone the girls.

The solution to the cash problem was solved by putting jars at the store and Chez Buffet. Both jars came with neatly printed signs that read:

Please help our Graduates
Enjoy an enlightening, educational experience
We Are The Future!

They "salted" each jar with a fifty-cent piece and hoped others would take the hint. It took about a month to get enough money in the jars for the trip. Muckluckers were generous, especially when it came to their kids.

The day of the Senior Skip arrived amid great excitement. We set off early on that beautiful, warm, clear June morning so we could have more time in the "big city."

The kids had scrounged old mattresses, pillows and sleeping bags to cushion the ride in the back of the trucks. The boys and Orvill rode with Felix Carrington, while the girls and I made ourselves as comfortable as possible in Bob Dodson's truck bed.

We weren't settled in long before Felix's truck blew a tire. Only half a mile out of town, our little procession came to a halt and we disembarked.

Felix located the spare tire, but he couldn't find the jack. Unbelievably, Bob didn't have one either.

Felix took one of the boys for company, and they loped off toward town. Soon they were back with a jack and a picnic basket of food that we'd forgotten at Esther's place.

Although we'd all had breakfast, we found tire changing to be hungry work. So we polished off the picnic then and there, enjoying fried Spam and mayo sandwiches, deviled eggs, pickles, and gooseberry tarts — all washed down with cold, clear creek water. Delicious!

We climbed on board the trucks again and set off. I don't know what the boys talked about, but the girls discussed movie stars, clothes and boys. They all were mad for Cary Grant and declared Clark Gable to be a bit old, but still dreamy "in a scary kind of way."

The girls thought Van Johnson was cute, "like the boy next door," and Alan Ladd was interesting, but too short. They weren't fond of Shirley Temple, either, because their mothers used her as the example of "the perfect young lady." All of them sighed longingly that they would simply die to look like Lana Turner or Rita Hayworth.

They must have got their movie star information from magazines, for we sure didn't have a theater in Muckluck. I didn't have much to add to the conversation, as I didn't read movie mags. Privately, though, I thought Clark Gable could park his butt on my sofa any day, even if he was a bit long in the tooth.

We stopped at beautiful Summit Lake to enjoy the scenery and eat the fudge Ronald's mother had sent along. It felt wonderful to stretch our legs and "visit Mrs. Jones." That was easy for the boys, but the girls and I had to find heavy brush for cover. It took a while. We were very modest.

Speaking of Summit Lake, I remember one year during rutting season when I saw two bull moose engaged in battle over a female. They were at the edge of the lake, battling it out with antlers crashing.

It sounded like gun-fire resounding off the surrounding mountains. They must have become exhausted, because after one enormous clash, their antlers locked together. Try as they might, they couldn't separate. I suppose they starved to death, for their remains were found a few days later, still locked in combat.

Well, back to my story. After we had taken care of our business, we got back on the road and headed for Seward. Then Felix pulled over again and his boys climbed out of the truck.

Ronald's face was pea-soup green. He was carsick. And he'd managed to throw up all over Buz and Arnie. Luckily, we were near a stream. So the boys washed up as best they could, and soon we hit the road again. Time was a-wasting.

We had one more stop to make, however. Everyone wanted to meet legendary Alaska Nellie Lawing.

That woman had her own museum, wrote her autobiography and entertained visitors who stopped by often to hear tales of her fascinating, rugged life. You might have heard of her. She was famous.

Alaska Nellie gave the boys some soap and hot water, and they became presentable once more. We'd have stayed all day visiting with her, but we knew we had to cram as much as possible into our brief Skip.

Although it was only 50 miles or so to Seward, it was mid-afternoon by the time we arrived on the outskirts of town. For all the excitement the Senior Skip generated, you'd think we were visiting a huge city. Actually, Seward only claimed around 1,500 people in those days. But compared to Muckluck, it was big time. Our young country bumpkins were thrilled to be leaving "boring old Muckluck" far behind.

We passed the Jesse Lee Home for children and the Territorial School. Then we drove straight down Fourth Avenue, Seward's Broadway, to the docks. The kids wanted to see Resurrection Bay.

We were lucky. In the distance, we saw an orca breaching, and then two eagles soared over the water. Some otters were playing near shore, too.

Resurrection Bay is an ice-free port all year around. It is absolutely gorgeous, with nearby snowy mountains reflected in its deep-blue water. If there's a prettier spot in the world, I haven't seen it yet.

Alaska Steam's *Baranoff* was in port. It was the biggest and grandest ship the kids and I had ever seen and was nearly as fascinating as the Bay itself. We watched the longshoremen unload cargo, until we reluctantly pulled ourselves away for more adventure.

Leaving the pickups with their owners, we strolled up Fourth, stopping at Brown and Hawkins department store. We marveled at the abundance of merchandise they stocked. In the Alaska Shop, we saw Alaska-made items offered for sale.

We were thrilled to find some of Dave Moffid's carved wood critters featured. And we let everyone within earshot know we were "tight" with the artist.

Then we found a little Italian restaurant that offered big platters of spaghetti at a price we could afford, and we wolfed it down. Sylvia's provided ice cream cones for dessert, both chocolate and vanilla.

Our last treat for the evening was a movie at the Liberty Theater. *The Bells of St. Mary's* with Bing Crosby and Ingrid Bergman was playing. I remember thinking it was a fitting film for the kids to enjoy.

Well, the girls enjoyed it anyway. I think the boys got a little restless, and some time during the show James slipped outside. We novice chaperones didn't even miss him. Well, it was dark in there.

James, determined to have a more memorable Senior Skip than we'd managed thus far, soon met three Seward gals out for a stroll. He invited himself along and, of course, the girls thought he was just the cutest thing.

To cut to the chase — as James did — James soon found himself in the back of Felix's truck with a flirt named Shelly. It was James' misfortune that he chose to romance the only child of Seward's chief of police.

The chief just happened to be patrolling when he saw his pride and joy, the lovely Shelly, boosted into a truck shell by a stranger.

The other two girls ran and hid. The chief hurried over to Felix's truck and quietly opened the little door to the shell. He shined his flashlight on the interior and found our young Romeo with his hands where they ought not to have been. You'll have to use your imagination.

The chief grabbed James by the ear and hauled him to the ground. A tearful Shelly was ordered home to her mother, and James was escorted to the station house. It seems that Shelly was only 15 years old.

Well, when Orvill and I noticed that James was among the missing, we left the theater with the remnant of our senior class and began searching for our wayward teenager. I don't mind telling you, I was worried. After all, I was supposed to be keeping a sharp eye on the Skippers, and now one had skipped out. Orvill admitted he was having similar concerns.

It still was quite light out, but the streets weren't busy. Most of Seward was tucked away for the night.

Then one of our kids found Shelly's girlfriends who, while blubbering and sniffing, tried to explain what had happened. We eventually got the gist of the story.

Leading our little flock of scared, embarrassed and intimidated yokels, we arrived at the station house. After several hours of explaining, pleading and promises from Orvill and me, and a few tears on James' part, the chief cooled down and agreed to let James go in our custody.

I've often wondered if Orvill might have slipped "something" into the chief's pocket. But I didn't ask and he didn't tell — and I would not cast aspersions on the chief, you may be sure.

We'd planned on renting two rooms at the Van Gilder Hotel. One for the guys and one for the girls and myself. We'd figured there wouldn't be enough beds for everyone, so we came prepared with the sleeping bags. But by the time we got to the hotel, it was well past midnight and our rooms were occupied.

We were shocked at the prices they had posted on the wall. Turns out that we couldn't have afforded the rooms anyway.

With the spaghetti feed, the ice cream cones and the movie, we'd used up most of our money. If we'd saved that picnic basket for dinner, as intended, we would have been "in the money," but hindsight never does anybody any good now, does it?

So we headed to the trucks and bedded down on the mattresses. I didn't sleep much that night, and when I finally dozed off, my dreams were disturbing. I felt like a chaperone failure.

We'd planned on doing more sightseeing the next morning, but a unanimous vote showed we were tired of Skipping. Everyone was ready to return to good, old, familiar, safe Muckluck. We bade farewell to the big city, and with sighs of relief, set our faces toward home, sweet home.

That was the first and last Senior Skip for Muckluck graduates.

I'll bet you're getting tired of my yammering by now. You're not?

Well, it's time for my pills, so why don't you run along and do something productive for a while. If you want to hear more about Muckluck's heyday, drop in again next Sunday afternoon. I usually feel like talking on Sundays after church, and I've got lots more tales to tell if you want to hear 'em.

~ 23 ~

Well, here you are again. Ready for more Muckluck tales? Okay, make yourself at home and prop your ears open. I've been wracking my brain to remember some of the more interesting happenings, and bless me, there's still plenty to tell.

I especially like this next one. It happened the year after our Senior Skip experience, when we learned that James wasn't the only Romeo running around loose.

Two weeks before Valentine's Day, Molly Parkins got a big surprise. Maybe I should say she received a big shock.

It all started as she was sorting incoming mail. Molly came across an envelope addressed to her. It's not as if she never got any mail, but it was a jolt to see a letter actually addressed to *her*.

She finished sorting other people's letters, put a few catalogs notices in the proper boxes, and tidied up the smelly, stiff canvas mailbag before she turned to her own correspondence.

She liked to prolong the suspense. In fact, she went into her quarters, poured herself a well-deserved cup of coffee and settled down in her easy chair before she took up the envelope and slit the end with a paring knife.

She blew it open with a puff and peeked inside. It wasn't a letter, it was a card.

"Well," thought Molly, "it's not my birthday, and it's not Christmas. What's this all about?"

As we know, Molly was not one to rush through things. She liked to take her time and enjoy the experience. She put her feet up on the footstool and sipped her coffee while she pondered.

At last she cautiously removed the card from the envelope. It was a beautiful valentine, a fancy one with paper lace, cupids, hearts and flowers. It was homemade, too.

Molly's eyes grew wide. Her breath came in short gasps and her heart started beating faster.

"What the Sam Hill is this supposed to mean?" she wondered, as she slowly opened the card and read the carefully printed words.

"You are my soul's desire.
You set my heart afire.
Please give me a sign
And say you'll be mine."

There was no signature.

"Whoa, there," Molly muttered. "This is not Robert Browning, but it ain't all bad either. Who in the world could it be from?"

Molly spent the rest of the day, evening and most of the night thinking about that valentine and the unknown poet.

I happened to stop by the post office the next day, and there was Molly, sitting on a high stool in front of the little customer window, gazing into space as though she were in a trance. I spoke to her twice before she noticed I'd come through the door. She had a white envelope in her hand.

"Oh, hi Kate. When did you come in?" She looked bemused, pixilated. "Do you have time for a cup or two? I've got some fresh-baked strudel in the kitchen."

I'm not going to turn down coffee or strudel, so I walked 'round to her kitchen door and let myself in. Molly came in from the post office in the next room.

She poured two cups of steaming coffee, then cut and plated the strudel and put forks on the table. All the time she kept that envelope in her hand.

"Uh, Molly," I began, "What's that you're holding onto so tight? I hope it's not bad news."

Molly looked at me as if I had two heads.

"No, of course not. In fact, it's rather nice news," she said, as she pushed the envelope across the table. "Here, take a gander at this."

I noticed it was postmarked from Anchorage, so it must have come via train to Seward and then to Muckluck on Izzy's weekly truck route. I pulled the card out and opened it.

"It's very pretty, but it's not signed," I noted. "Who's it from?"

"I haven't the faintest," Molly said, as she pursed her lips and frowned. "But I'd sure give a pretty penny to know!"

I was floored. We chewed on ideas as to the sender while we ate the strudel. Ever so often the little bell on the door of the post office would ring when someone came in, and Molly would go take care of business. When she returned, we talked some more about the mysterious admirer.

But we never got beyond being totally stumped. Eventually, I had to get home and start dinner, so I left Molly staring into space, still looking dumbstruck.

Several days passed before I saw her again. She was coming out of Chez Buffet, and she still had a white envelope in her hand. I wondered if she carried it with her everywhere she went.

But no, this was a different envelope. Inside was another valentine, which was even more flowery than the first. Molly pulled me along to her place, where we finished off the strudel. It was a little stale, but we dunked it in coffee and it was fine.

While we relished the treat, I read the new card.

> *"You're in my thoughts both night and day.*
> *I only wish that you would say*
> *That you would be my valentine.*
> *Please tell me, Dear, that you'll be mine."*

"Criminey Molly, this guy's got it bad!" I read the poem several times.

"Don't I know it! I never had anybody say things like that to me, and I don't know what to think," she said. "To tell the truth, I'm kinda flattered. But what if it's just a mean joke?"

"Oh, I don't think it's a joke," I told her. "Somebody put a lot of work into these cards, and I think he's on the level.

I looked up at Molly. She just sat there and chewed on her bottom lip.

"You should be flattered," I said. "It's not every day a gal gets valentines as passionate as these two."

"I know, I know ... but what should I do?"

Molly ran her fingers through her graying hair. She was beginning to look seriously disturbed.

"Lady, you are barking up the wrong tree," I said as I shook my head. "I'm sure not the one to ask about romance. The last man I kissed was my pa, and he's been dead for nine years. Maybe you should talk to Olav."

Olav was the problem solver for Muckluckers. It was only natural to turn to him in our quandary.

"Oh, I couldn't! I mean, what if it's him? Even if it's not him, I'd be too embarrassed!"

Molly wrung her hands and looked about to cry. She twisted her hanky and spilled coffee on the oilcloth.

"Well, don't fret about it, Moll, there's nothing to worry about. It's not as if he sounds dangerous. In fact, it's plain to see that he's smitten with you."

I then told her to be patient. I was sure our mystery man would show his hand shortly.

But he didn't. In fact, two days before Valentine's Day, another card came for Molly. After receiving it, she locked up the post office and hurried through the snow to my cabin.

I'd just finished scrubbing the linoleum, so she took off her boots before shedding her jacket and then sat down at my table. I was fresh out of baked goods, so I offered Graham crackers with our coffee. We broke the crackers into two bowls, soaked them with canned milk, and poured on a spoonful of sugar. They actually tasted pretty good.

Molly was more shaken than ever as she handed me her new envelope. The poet had decorated this card with pictures cut from a magazine and drawn hearts around them with a red pencil. It was not as fancy as the others, but it looked more serious somehow.

Sure enough, there was another poem inside.

You are my bright and shining star
I've loved you — always from afar.
You'd bring pure joy into my life
If you would only be my wife.

My Great Aunt Hannah, this was more serious. This was a bona-fide proposal!

"This is the first proposal I've ever had in all my forty-seven years," Molly wailed. "And I don't even know who the man is."

I tried my best to calm her, but I certainly could appreciate her frustration. After all, this fella might be an axe murderer or a shyster. Or even a Communist.

I advised Molly to just be careful and keep a watchful eye out for clues. I offered to stay with her, but she said she had a loaded pistol nearby at all times. And she knew how to use it. I'd seen her take target practice out at the town dump.

We had a dusting of snow the night of February 13. In the morning, Molly went out to sweep the snow off her path and porch. Her eyes nearly popped out of her head when she found a pink box tied in a big, pink ribbon sitting on the porch just outside the door. She carefully picked it up and listened to see if it was ticking. Nope, no ticking, so it probably wasn't a bomb.

She dropped her broom and carried the box gingerly into her house. She placed it on the kitchen table and studied it closely. It was smaller than a breadbox, but bigger than a cake pan. She looked out the window and saw me passing by on my way to the school where Thelma was holding a Valentine's Day party for the kids.

In those days, our valentines were all handmade. Each kid in school had spent weeks making valentines, and every single child was sure to get his or her fair share. Each student decorated a box, usually a shoe box, with tissue or crepe paper. Then they glued all the lace, ribbon, romantic pictures and any fancy do-lolly they could find all over it. A wide slit cut in the lid made it the perfect "mailbox" for their valentines.

I enjoyed being part of the fun. But as I sloshed my way toward the school, Molly hailed me. I detoured into her kitchen and was as surprised as she was to see that pretty pink box now sitting on her table.

"Did you open it yet?" I asked.

"Nope, I'm scared to," Molly whispered.

"Well, I'm not!" I slid the big pink ribbon off the box and lifted the lid. Inside was a bright red heart-shaped box with crimped lace around the edge. I sniffed the box like a hunting dog and smelled — chocolate. Under the fancy lid lay five pounds of chocolate candy, no doubt from Sylvia's shop in Seward. I'm not fibbing. Five pounds of assorted chocolate candies, each in its own tiny, gold, pleated cup.

Molly gasped and clapped her hand to her mouth.

I drooled. I hate to admit it, but I did. You know I love baked goods of all kinds, but store-bought chocolates are such a treat.

After several moments of admiring the delightful treasure, Molly remembered her manners.

"Won't you have a piece, Kate?" she asked, strangely stiff and polite.

I believe she thought the occasion demanded decorum on her part. I didn't wait for a second invitation. I dug right in and popped one of the candies into my mouth. Oh boy, talk about lucky — I got a chocolate-covered cherry. My favorite!

Molly helped herself to a piece and was rewarded with chocolate, caramel and crushed nuts. We each sampled half a dozen more before I came to my senses and put the lid back on the box. We might have kept on gobbling all day if somebody didn't call a halt.

We just sat at the table looking at that red heart-shape box, licking our lips and wondering what to do next.

"It's from him," Molly finally said.

"Of course, it's from him," I agreed. "But who *is* he?"

Just then the bell rang in the post office. I followed right behind Molly and we greeted Olav.

"Hey," he said with a grin. "I can see by the mess on your faces that you got the box of candy Izzy left at your door this morning."

Izzy? Izzy Fitzheimer? Izzy was Molly's secret admirer, the man who wrote those atrocious poems and who had asked her to marry him? I don't know who was more surprised, Molly or me. But I know who was more pleased.

Molly had long had a crush on Izzy. Each week when he brought the mail from Seward, he stopped in for coffee and cookies or a piece of cake. He and Molly had enjoyed each other's company for years.

They laughed at each other's jokes and exchanged the week's happenings. Izzy had been kind and consoling when Mr. Parkins, Molly's pa, passed away. Yet somehow neither had ever guessed at the direction their friendship was heading. Love is blind in more ways than one.

When the whole story came out, it was perfectly obvious. Olav had hitched a ride with Izzy to Seward the week before and saw him buy the candy at Sylvia's. He'd also been looking out his window at 5:30 a.m. and saw Izzy sneak up to Molly's door with the big, pink box in his hands.

It didn't take a genius to figure out what was going on. Izzy must have mailed that first valentine while he was on business in Anchorage. And now Olav, who didn't know about the valentines, didn't realize he was spilling the beans. But by our surprised — and in Molly's case, delighted — expressions, he sure knew he'd blown Izzy's cover.

I tended the post office the rest of that day, while Molly rushed over to Izzy's place to give him her breathless, "Yes!"

When she came back, she was smiling from ear to ear. And I was going to be a bridesmaid once again.

Molly and I each had three more pieces of candy to go with our coffee, and we began planning the wedding.

A Valentine To My Love

I wrote this Valentine to say
You mean the world to me.
My love for you is bright as day
And endless as the sea.

If you will walk beside me
I shall have no need of fears
For I know your love will guide me
As the days turn into years.

My love was never stronger
Than it is for you today,
And each day this love increases
So there's nothing more to say....

Except "I think you're wonderful.
I thank God you are mine.
My fervent prayer is that you'll always
Be my Valentine!"

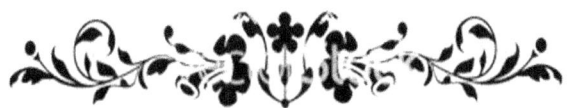

~ 24 ~

It may seem to you that Muckluckers spent a lot of time on festivals, pageants and general tomfoolery. In our defense, I must remind you that we had little entertainment in those days. We didn't have movies, television, Disneyland, star-studded concerts or any other amusements folks enjoy today. We had to make our own fun.

Holidays were very important to us. We made the most of Christmas, Easter, Halloween and Valentine's Day. But one of our most favorite holidays was the Fourth of July. Alaskans have always been proud to be Americans — even if, as a territory, we were only stepchildren of the United States.

"That's okay," we'd say proudly. "Who needs statehood? Maybe it'll come some day, but we're doing fine just as we are!" And we meant it.

So we always went all out on July 4. Every home displayed a 48-star flag, some small, homemade efforts and some large, store-bought banners. Ribbons of bunting graced the post office and school house. We tidied our yards and donned our best clothes.

Usually there was a combination baseball game and box social, along with plenty of other merriments. One year especially stands out in my memory.

The fun started in the schoolyard at noon. We began with gunnysack races. First the grade-school kids, then the high-school students, and finally the adults. It was fun to watch folks race along, with the lower halves of their bodies stuffed into burlap bags. They had to hold on tight to the harsh fabric to keep the sacks from falling off. Racers hopped, waddled, fell and rolled until one crossed the finish line and won the blue ribbon.

The three-legged race followed. Couples tied one of their legs to one of their partner's legs. They took off as fast as they could go when the whistle blew. It was rib-splitting funny, 'cause some of the partners were very strangely matched. For instance, Betty Roundtree ran with her eight-year-old son. He was so fast that he had to drag her most of the way.

Olav and Benny ran together, but both wanted to set the pace. They ended up on the ground more often than not. Rotund Chef Buffet chose equally chubby Nanny Burrows as his running mate. We were in stitches. I ran with Father Sorinoff, but his long robe kept tripping me up. The teenagers wisely chose each other and, of course, their most coordinated couple won the ribbon.

The egg race came last. We used raw eggs and tablespoons. Two teams, each made up of eight people, were given a raw egg and a tablespoon. At the whistle, the first person from each team ran, balancing the egg on his spoon, to the school house steps and back. Then he had to pass the egg, without touching it with his hand, to the next person in line. That teammate then ran to the steps and back to the third person — and so on until one team finished first.

Along the way, eggs dropped and splattered, making the way to the steps slimy and slippery. We howled with laughter as Nanny, still game, slipped, skidded a few feet and then sat down on her well-padded behind in a splat of raw egg. Nanny laughed the hardest.

It's a shame people don't play those games any more. Nowadays everybody seems strung so tight that they don't know how to relax and have fun. Folks would rather be "spectators" than get out there and play. They're missing out on a lot of laughs, and some good exercise, too. Now they pay big money to belong to a gym, whereas we got all the exercise we needed — for free — just working and playing.

The races took about an hour, so there was plenty of time for the softball game that followed. Teams were made up of grown men versus high school boys.

We had a couple ash bats and several balls, but only five mitts. Those went to the catcher and the four in-fielders. Everybody else had to make do with their bare hands.

The bases were hand-sewn with fishing line and several layers of sturdy canvas. They were stuffed with dried grass.

The game was a regular barn-burner. Faithful fans of both teams screamed their lungs out. The score was 12 to 8 in the third inning, with the men's team in the lead.

Sophomore Homer Waldorf was manning third base when Felix hit a pop-up straight at him. Homer backed up, squinted into the sun, and held his glove in the air.

He had it! Oops. The ball hit the glove, bounced off and dropped to the ground. Felix was safe on first. The younger crowd groaned in agony, and poor Homer hung his head. The game went on.

The boys were losing by two runs and were at bat in the bottom of the ninth inning. The score was 20 to 18, with boys on second and third base. Young Homer stepped up and took the bat. Still smarting from dropping the ball, you could see the scowl on his red face.

He was not a particularly good hitter, but we knew he'd do his level best to redeem himself. Two balls and two strikes later, it looked like the game was over. It seemed destined that the men would take the wooden trophy, carved by Dave Moffid.

The pitcher, Charlie Martin from Martin's Saw Mill, wound up and let fly. Homer connected with that bullet and knocked it into the woods. The two boys already on base tore up home plate with Homer right behind 'em.

The game was over. The lads had won, and Homer Waldorf was the hero of the day. He was carried off the field on his teammates' shoulders. His face was still red, but the scowl was gone, replaced by the biggest grin you ever saw.

After the game it was time for the box social. If you've never participated in a box social, you don't know what you've been missing.

The women and older girls had decorated cardboard boxes any way they fancied. Some were sweet and frilly, while others were more masculine with cut-outs of hunting scenes, fish or moose pictures taken from magazines. After the boxes were decorated, they were filled with every kind of delicious edible we could concoct, including chicken pot pies, moose meatloaf, bacon and egg sandwiches, or fried chicken.

Side dishes like coleslaw, twice-baked potatoes, deviled eggs, potato salad and baked beans were tossed in, too. As for dessert, oh my. The boxes contained German chocolate cake, rhubarb pie, wild berry tarts or brownies. And much, much more.

Each box was held up for inspection, but the contents and the cooks were kept secret. Then the bidding began. The highest bidder got that box. And the privilege of eating supper with the lady who brought it. It was so much fun — the suspense, surprises and delight or disappointment, always well disguised.

One of the Raben twins, I never could tell them apart, won me and my box. We were both satisfied, if not exactly thrilled. Breaking the gender rules, Chef Buffet had entered a box, and when Benny Carson won that box of gourmet delights *and* Chef Buffet, he declared he was a most fortunate fella. He already had Violet to go home with, and the contents of the box more than made up for the lack of female companionship at supper.

Those not wanting to go the box social route brought their own picnics, so everyone was well fed, fat and happy. The money raised from the social was used to buy materials for playground equipment for the kiddos.

Then it was time for the Miss Liberty Contest.

Contestants were limited to any unmarried woman in town. That included Carol and me, as well as several other spinsters, and all the high school girls. I was dead set against entering what amounted to a beauty contest. But Carol, as usual, dragged me along. I liked to think of myself as a good sport.

We ladies lined up on the school steps, each holding a large number and posing prettily. Small pieces of paper were passed out to the crowd. Then folks wrote the number of their favorite and placed the slips in Bing Sultz's hat. Bing and Father Sorinoff were in charge of counting the votes.

When the winner was announced, she was presented with a blue ribbon and a spiked crown made out of tinfoil-covered cardboard fashioned to look like the crown worn by the Statue of Liberty.

Seventeen-year-old Marie Dodson won the crown that year, and a very pretty Miss Liberty she was, too.

But that's when the trouble started. As sometimes happened, a carload of boys from Seward had crashed our party. They behaved themselves right up to the end, watching the fun from the sidelines. Then one of the boys decided to take liberties with Miss Liberty.

Marie was dating the Middleton boy, who stepped in to defend his girl. Words were exchanged and some pushing followed. Before we knew it, there was a first-class donnybrook going on between the Seward boys and our Muckluck teens, and some beefy punches were thrown. There were a couple of nosebleeds, and two or three puffy eyes, before Olav got control. With the help of Mr. Martin, the marshal broke up the fight.

Olav told the Seward boys they could either spend the night locked up in our jail or get on back to Seward immediately. The boys didn't know we didn't have a jail, but the thought of being locked up anywhere in Muckluck didn't appeal to them. They skedaddled back to their home territory.

Miss Liberty kissed her battered hero, accidentally knocking her crown off in the process.

We built a huge bonfire in the middle of the road and sat around swapping stories, singing and watching the sparks fly toward the sky. When the fire was well burned out, and soaked with buckets of water from Moose Run, we picked up the litter in the schoolyard, packed our belongings, and made our way to our cozy beds. Happy Independence Day. God bless America!

~ 25 ~

A few years after the war — I'm talking about World War II now — we began getting letters from European aristocrats seeking hunting guides. They explained that Allied bombs had not only destroyed most of Europe, including their hunting lodges, but most of the wild animals, too.

Now they were rebuilding their lodges and needed trophies to decorate their walls. Nothing ever came from most of that correspondence, so either the lodge owners changed their minds or found guides elsewhere.

But one letter did bring a foreigner to our soil, and that's a story no Mucklucker will ever forget.

As I've told you, we had a couple fellas in town who qualified as big game guides. So whenever a foreign-looking envelope with an interesting stamp came to the post office, Molly handed it over to either Wild Bill Hansen or Joe Sterns, depending on who needed a job the most.

This particular time Joe was working at the saw mill, so Wild Bill got the letter. He showed it around town, impressing us with the artful penmanship as much as the signature of Count Stanislaus Zewlinkoffsky of Warsaw, Poland. He'd heard of the fabulous hunting opportunities on the Kenai Peninsula and was looking for the best guide money could hire. He wanted moose, bear and goat trophies.

At the mention of money, Wild Bill perked up and immodestly declared he fit the bill. Thelma helped him write to the Count, saying he'd happily guide him to some "magnificent animals."

It took several months of back and forth letter exchanges, but finally a date was set in October. Bill advised the Count to bring heavy clothes, including rain gear, a warm hat, sturdy boots and plenty of money.

Let me put in my two cents here — in those days, hunting was considered a perfectly reasonable and necessary activity. We always needed meat, obviously, and since there were no Safeway or Costco stores around, we had to hunt and kill animals.

But there were folks then, and there are many more now, who consider killing anything with a face to be a travesty, if not a mortal sin. And there were people then, as now, who especially despised the killing of animals just for the trophies.

They are sickened by the sight of mounted heads on wood-paneled walls, or bear skin rugs laying on parquet floors. I tend to agree with them regarding hunting strictly for trophies. One can only hope the meat from the slain animals is used as food, as well. I'm no expert on what goes on in the hunting world any more, but I have my opinions.

Count Zewlinkoffsky made it clear he wanted a "real Alaskan experience," with none of the pampering he'd heard some guides provided. He knew a friend who had hunted in the Interior, who brought along his valet, cook and weapons expert. You can just imagine what he expected of his guide. Spoiled old gink! None of that for the Count —the rougher the better for him.

That suited Wild Bill. As his name suggests, he liked things wild and wooly. He had several horses in a corral out by Mud Lake, and he owned all the paraphernalia needed for campfire cooking. Nothing fancy, but good, sturdy iron pots and pans.

He decided not to provide tents, but to let the Count rough it in a sleeping bag on spruce boughs, under the wide, Alaska sky. If it was good enough for Wild Bill, it was good enough for Count Zewlinkoffsky.

On the appointed day, a chartered helicopter flew the Count from Seward. He'd had a long trip from Poland to Seattle to Seward, and finally, to Muckluck. Practically the whole town trotted out to the schoolyard to greet the visiting aristocrat.

We were mighty impressed as he jumped from the helicopter, ducked under the rotor blades and marched over to Olav. The marshal was standing stiffly beside Wild Bill, who was slouching in his usual manner. Highfalutin' titles did not impress Bill. But then nothing impressed him, except maybe a freak of nature like an albino moose or a tailless beaver, both of which he claimed to have seen, believe it or not.

The Count was tall and trim. He sported a large mustache and a nicely coordinated European hunting costume made up of a heavy, brown jacket with lots of pockets, jodhpurs, a wool cap and shoepacks. His posture was outstanding, his blue eyes alert.

The pilot unloaded several serious-looking rifles and a couple of boxes before lifting off, leaving us windblown and speechless. I'd never seen Olav at a loss for words. But he was originally from a country that respected its royalty, so you can understand his feelings.

Wild Bill didn't have that upbringing. He stuck out a dirty, rough paw and practically shook the Count's arm off. The Count gave as good as he got. They were an odd looking pair, but the men seemed compatible.

The rest of us lined up to meet and greet our important visitor. Some of us shook his hand, a few of the women even dipped tight curtseys. The Count smiled warmly and spoke remarkably good English with only a slight accent. He explained that as a boy he had had a British tutor who taught him the King's English.

Wild Bill and a couple of the boys picked up the boxes and weapons. They then set off for Chez Buffet, where the men dined royally on moose steaks, julienne creamed carrots, sourdough rolls, garlic mashed potatoes and berry pie.

With full bellies, they headed out to Bill's cabin to spend the night. The next morning, they took off into the mountains on horseback, leading a spare pack horse.

I can't tell you how the hunt went, but I do know that after a few days Wild Bill returned to town for more supplies. He said they were tracking a brown bear that, from the size of his paw prints, "looks to be a big'un."

The guide reported that the Count was a good sport. He didn't complain about the lack of comforts or the occasional rain.

Actually, Wild Bill considered him a gentleman. The Count didn't talk a lot, cleaned up his own messes and was, in Bill's opinion, tolerable company. The men had shot a few spruce hens, cooked them on sticks over the campfire, and had found some wild strawberries for their hotcakes.

The next time Wild Bill came to town, he said they'd killed a moose with a six-foot spread. The Count was delighted. Bill said they'd be packing it out and divvying up the meat with the locals before returning to look for the bear and goat. He picked up more supplies and took off up and over the mountains again.

That afternoon, a message came from Anchorage that shocked Olav. He banged on his window and beckoned me to come in when I strolled past his cabin on my way to the store.

"What's wrong?" I asked when I saw his distress.

Olav was standing there holding a message that he'd just recieved via radio. You see, Olav had acquired a wireless radio transmitter a while back and he was able to send and receive messages from the main station in Anchorage.

When a message arrived for a Mucklucker, Olav would copy it down and deliver it. And when one of us needed to send a message, Olav was happy to oblige. It didn't happen often, but we appreciated the convenience.

Well, he was in quite a dither over this recent transmission.

"Take a gander at this!" Olav said, as he shook his head and handed me a slip of paper on which he'd written an incoming message.

> URGENT! The Anchorage Bureau of Investigation has reason to believe a suspected Nazi war criminal is hiding on the Kenai Peninsula. Federal marshals will be in your area soon, along with Nazi hunter Izadore Weimer. The suspect is using the alias Count Zewlinkoffsky. He is known to be armed and extremely dangerous. If seen, do not attempt to confront or apprehend this man. More to follow.

"Jumpin' Jehoshaphat!" I cried. "If that doesn't take the cake."

Olav and I stared at each other, our mouths hanging open. Nothing like that had ever happened in Muckluck.

We poured ourselves cups of hot coffee and just sat and thought for a while. We kept staring at each other, shaking our heads. I remember my hands were shaking, too, and Olav kept clearing his throat nervously.

We figured Wild Bill would be bringing the moose meat to town soon, with or without the Count. Then Olav could get Bill alone and show him the message. We vowed to keep mum in the meantime. Believe me, it wasn't easy keeping a secret of that magnitude, but we managed.

Wild Bill arrived on his horse later that day, leading the pack horse. Both animals bore sacks of meat, which Bill dumped at the store for distribution.

Olav had been keeping a watchful eye, so he rushed over and pulled Wild Bill aside. He then escorted Bill to his cabin, where he showed him the message. To say that Wild Bill was dumbstruck would be a gross understatement.

"What should I do?" Bill stammered. "I could go back and shoot him dead if you just give the say-so."

"No, that's no good," Olav told him. "Can't have you arrested for murder."

The marshal explained that the situation had to be handled in a legal way, with the authorities making the capture and taking the Count into custody.

"We've just got to act normal and not spill the beans in any way," Olav said. "You're the only person who knows where he is, so here's what I've come up with."

Olav told Wild Bill to gather a few more supplies and head back to the camp. When the Count fell asleep that night, Wild Bill was to bring all three horses back to town.

"That'll put a knot in his tail. He has no idea where he is, and he'll be wondering what happened to you and the horses," Olav told him.

"I'm betting he trusts you and will just sit tight waiting for you to come back," Olav added.

According to a second message, the authorities would be in Muckluck the next day. Olav thought Wild Bill could lead them to the camp and sneak up on the Nazi.

"D'ya think that'll work?" Wild Bill asked.

Well, Olav wasn't completely convinced himself, but it was the best he could come up with on short notice.

Wild Bill still insisted he should shoot the S.O.B. and say it was an accident, but Olav stuck to his guns. And so they had a plan.

Sure enough, the next day here came two U.S. marshals and Mr. Izadore Weimer. He was a Jewish man who had been hunting Nazis in Argentina — and had trailed this one, Herr Wilhelm Krongaus, to Muckluck.

Mr. Weimer was a small man with a big score to settle. He'd lost most of his family in the Holocaust. We Muckluckers considered him a hero, and we wished him good luck and God speed in his honorable search.

The three men set off on horseback, along with Wild Bill and Olav. They traveled up and over the mountain range.

I guess the capture went smoothly, for by nightfall they were back. Herr Krongaus was in handcuffs and tied behind one of the marshals. He didn't look so blamed cocky anymore, and his former welcoming committee stood silent and angry. Muckluck had lost a couple fine soldier boys during the war, and another came home missing a leg.

We learned later that Herr Krongaus was tried and convicted of unspeakable crimes. He had been the commandant of one of the death camps in Poland. He was hanged, and we were happy. He got what was coming to him.

We were proud of our part in seeing justice done. We actually hoped more Nazis would show up so we could do the right thing.

~ 26 ~

Most of the time, Muckluckers moseyed along in blissful tranquility, but we did have our moments. Like the time when things in the Shultz household weren't going so well.

Although the store was doing fine, Bing and Val were having "marital problems." They'd been married twenty-seven years, raised two fine children and owned a profitable store for eight years. I think this was around 1945 or so.

Folks enjoyed dropping in at the store to exchange news — and sometimes downright gossip. Older fellas liked to sit around the woodstove, warming their feet, telling lies and laughing at each other's stale jokes. The spit can was always close at hand.

Women sometimes brought a list for Bing or Val to fill while they ran other errands. And the Sultzes didn't mind tending a kid or two when the occasion called for it. I often wandered over to the store just to have some company. Bing liked to talk fishing and Val just liked to talk.

And then, it seemed like out of the clear blue sky, things changed. Folks started noticing a different atmosphere in the store. Bing acted preoccupied and didn't tell jokes like he used to. Val looked peaked and didn't have much to say. The sourdoughs didn't feel so comfortable around the old black stove any more. Something foul was afoot. We talked about it among ourselves, but it took a while before the truth came out.

The Sultzes were talking about divorce.

"Oh, surely there must be some mistake," we told ourselves. "Not Bing and Val. They're just in the doldrums. They'll snap out of it one of these days."

But they didn't snap out of it. They tried, but the situation got progressively worse. At first they just stopped speaking to one another. And then they started sniping at each other. On several occasions loud, angry voices were heard coming from their living quarters after the store was closed for the evening. We knew it wasn't any of our business, but doggone it, we loved them both and hated to see what was happening.

They tried to patch things up. They really did. First they went to Father Sorinoff for counseling. Sitting in his cozy little kitchen, they admitted they just weren't happy any more. They felt they would be better off to separate. What else could they do?

Poor Father! He'd never been married, although it was perfectly legal in his Russian Orthodox faith, and he really had no experience in marital problems. The best he could do was to tell them to try harder. He also promised to light candles and say prayers for them.

The next time Reverend Sneed came to town, they closed the store for an hour and button-holed him in their living room. He was as shocked and saddened at their news as any of us. And just about as helpful as Father Sorinoff.

Their problem really blindsided him, and the best advice he could offer up was, "the family that prays together, stays together." He advised them to stay and pray, and then he pleaded other commitments and fled.

Since Bing and Val had been staying and praying for twenty-seven years, it didn't seem to be working for them. Eventually, they separated. Val came to me and asked if she could bunk at my place until she figured out what to do next. I didn't want to take sides, but I couldn't turn her out either.

So I got a roommate. Val packed some of her clothes and lugged them to my place. She left everything else with Bing. Of course, they still had to see each other at the store every day, but with the new living arrangement, they were able to be civil to each other. Still, it was uncomfortable, to say the least.

Val and I spent many evenings drinking coffee and talking. That is, Val did the talking. To my discomfort, she shared her dissatisfaction of her husband with me.

Every evening she would play a variation of the same record. Bing was lazy. He would rather go fishing than tend the store. Bing wouldn't talk to her. He preferred talking with customers and the old geezers around the stove.

Bing wasn't brushing his teeth every day, and it drove her crazy to kiss him with Copenhagen on his breath. He chewed with his mouth open and clipped his toenails in bed. Bing stocked canned goods so high on the shelves she had to get a ladder to reach them. Bing wasn't making love to her any more.

Whoa! We were wading into deep water there, and I was getting quite uncomfortable. I squirmed and clenched my teeth so tight my jaw ached.

In an effort to get Val to stop vilifying Bing, I'd change the subject. But before you could say, "It looks like rain tomorrow," she was back on her favorite rant.

Finally, I just let her ramble on until it was bedtime. Then after crawling into bed, we would both have a restless night's sleep.

Val tossed and turned and often cried into her pillow. I just lay there miserable, hoping and praying something would change soon. I wanted Val and Bing to get back together so I could have my peaceful solitude again.

What I didn't know at the time was that Olav was having pretty much the same miseries with Bing. Although Bing was living in the Sultz quarters at the store, he spent evenings bending Olav's ear about the "shrew" he'd married.

Val just would not stop talking. She yapped all the time about silly stuff like clothes or articles she'd read in a magazine. She didn't want to talk about things that interested Bing. Things like fishing.

She hadn't learned any new recipes in the years they had been married. It was always the same old thing for supper — meatloaf and baked potatoes, spaghetti or moose stew. Bing wanted to go to Chez Buffet occasionally to try something different, but Val said it was a waste of money and wouldn't go.

Val nagged him about his personal hygiene. Imagine that!

It was his body, wasn't it? Val wanted more time off from the store to go and visit the grandkids in Seward. She splashed on way too much perfume and it aggravated his asthma. And on and on he went.

He nearly drove Olav to distraction, and Olav's well-known patience was wearing thin. When Bing started complaining that Val wasn't adventuresome in bed, Olav said he had to go do a nightly security check on the town, and left Bing to stew in his own juice.

Olav told me about this much later, after it was all over, and I told him my problems with Val. I've learned through many years of living that all things eventually come to an end, thank goodness.

This is how it happened.

I began to notice that Val wasn't eating much, but I chalked it up to her distress over the separation. Then she began to cough a lot. The coughing grew worse week by week, and then one day I noticed a bloody Kleenex in the wastebasket. That raised all kinds of red flags.

Tuberculosis was widespread in Alaska in those days, especially in the Native villages where people had little resistance to the disease. We Muckluckers had been lucky so far. But Val came into contact with lots of people at the store, visitors from everywhere, and she may have picked up the TB germ from one of them. I was scared for her. Heck, I was scared for *me*.

That evening we had a long, serious talk — and it wasn't about Bing for a change. Val insisted it was nothing and that she would feel better in a few days. I wanted her to go to a doctor in Seward for a checkup. She refused. I argued and pleaded, but it did no good. As we debated, Val began to cough. Bright, red blood stained her hanky.

That cinched it. I pulled out my big guns. If she didn't go see a doctor right away, she would have to move out of my home.

It was mean, and I felt like a heel, but it was the only thing that worked. We made arrangements to ride with Izzy on his next trip to Seward.

Izzy was suspicious, because we were so quiet on the ride. We preferred it that way, though, because we didn't want our fears to leak out. It was a long, miserable trip.

After examining Val, taking X-rays and running sputum tests, Dr. Balister told us the bad news. Val had TB. He wanted to put her in the Seward Sanitarium right then and there.

Val pleaded with the doctor to let her go back to Muckluck and settle a few things before being admitted. He agreed after we promised to be back in two days. We knew Izzy would make an extra trip once he knew the circumstances.

When we returned home, Val walked over to the store and told Bing she had tuberculosis. He was devastated. They cried and hugged and cried some more. And then they prayed together. Bing helped Val pack a few belongings.

Bing asked Esther Waldorf and me if we'd tend the store while he stayed in Seward during Val's treatment at the sanitarium. We didn't hesitate for a minute. Val had requested that the townsfolk be told of her disease, so they could be on the lookout.

When the news got around, everyone pitched in to help us at the store. And when I wasn't at the store, I had my cabin and bed all to myself. But I missed Val and worried about her all the time.

Townspeople sent many letters and cards to Val to cheer her up. Thelma had her students make get-well cards, and some of the women also sent little treats of jelly and cookies from time to time. Val was on a strict diet, but she was allowed a treat ever so often. Dr. Balister enjoyed his share of the goodies, too.

Treatment for TB was very different in those days. We didn't have all the drugs and therapies available today. Val dictated a letter to Bing that told us about her life in the sanitarium.

To All My Friends in Muckluck,

It appears I will be here from six to nine months if all goes well. It's the most boring existence you can ever imagine. I must have complete bed rest – no getting up except to go to the toilet once a day. (Thankfully, they have indoor bathrooms here. Ha!) I'm allowed to read, but can't do my "fancywork." I must lay flat except when propped up with pillows, and that only rarely. The window in the room, which I share with three other ladies, is open all day, as fresh air is believed to hasten the cure. We are given nourishing but boring meals. How my mouth waters for one of Chef Buffet's French creations! Even my own meatloaf would be welcome.

Dr. Balister says if all goes well I may be able to sit on a chair in a few weeks. Best of all, I may have a real bath after a month or so instead of the "spit baths" the nurses give several times a week. That will be heaven! Right now I'm leading the life of a log, but I am so grateful to be taken care of. Bing is my rock! He isn't allowed to visit every day, but he comes as often as they let him.

I thank you all for your letters, beautiful cards and prayers. Special thanks to those who are keeping the store going. You are saving our livelihood!

I send you all my love and big, warm hugs — Val

As things turned out, Val was able to come home after seven months at the sanitarium. She was instructed not to get tired and to stop whatever she was doing the minute she felt the least bit weary. It was hard to keep her down, but Bing and the rest of us kept a sharp eye on her.

It may be hard to believe, but the tuberculosis was a blessing in disguise. During their time in Seward, with Val trying so hard to stay quiet and remain still, and Bing scared spitless that he was going to lose her, they realized how foolish they had been to even think about divorce. They'd had time to talk over their differences and work out a way to improve themselves.

That experience was an eye-opener for a lot of Muckluckers. We began to count our blessings, forgive old hurts, and be, well, more loving and kind. Maybe that's one reason I remember Muckluck and its people with such fondness.

~ 27 ~

When Chez Buffet proved to be such a success, bringing people from all around the area to our town, a few ambitious folks thought Muckluck would be a fine place to start a business.

The first to come to town was Miss Alvira Goodrich. She arrived one day and moved into an abandoned building near the church. Oh my, but she was a case.

Her red hair, which she wore in a tall pile atop her head, made Carol's curls look faded. And her false eyelashes were so heavy, she could hardly keep her eyes open. She wore pancake makeup, stylish clothes and loads of jewelry. By Muckluck standards, she was the Queen of Sheba and Mae West rolled into one. We sat up and took notice.

Miss Alvira hired a couple young fellas to spruce up the place. She had them repair the roof, hook up a generator for electricity and paint everything inside and out. They painted it bright, bubblegum pink.

The next thing we knew, Izzy was bringing odd-looking furniture from Seward to fill the establishment. There was a chair that resembled a barber chair, a deep sink, several cabinets and a contraption that looked like a large football helmet on a metal stand. Soon, an eye-catching sign appeared over the front door.

MISS ALVIRA'S EMPORIUM OF BEAUTY

Well now, that had to be checked out. Carol and I were among the first customers, or clients, as Miss Alvira preferred to call us. We weren't sure what we wanted or needed, but decided we'd put ourselves in Miss Alvira's talented hands and hope for big improvements.

We just told her to take it easy and not get carried away. Miss Alvira set to work.

First she washed Carol's hair with some pungent, flowery smelling shampoo. While it dried, she washed mine. Then she put Carol in that odd chair and took up her scissors. Carol looked worried.

While my hair was drying, Miss Alvira set about removing Carol's shoulder-length curls. As each red curl fell to the floor, I thought "she's cutting a little close to the bone!"

But what did I know? I never was a beauty expert. Miss Alvira then mixed up a stinky concoction and applied it to what was left of Carol's hair. Whatever it was, it began stripping the henna right out. While that was "setting," she started in on me.

My hair was already rather short, but she hacked away confidently. Before I knew it, I had bangs. And a short Dutch-boy bob. What was left of my salt-and-pepper crop was slathered in black dye.

When Carol's hair was sufficiently stripped of color, it was miraculously turned into a platinum blonde color. After more washing, drying and trimming, little curlers appeared. Carol's head soon was covered with rollers, and she was looking nervous.

We took turns under the football helmet, which blew hot air onto our heads and nearly fried our ears. Miss Alvira checked from time to time to see if we were "done."

After a good four hours in the Emporium Of Beauty, it was time for the last comb out. We hadn't been allowed to see ourselves in the hand mirror during the procedure. But we did see each other, and we had sinking feelings that we'd made a big mistake.

Carol ended up looking like a white poodle, and I had become a chubby, middle-age Dutch lad with black hair and skimpy bangs. We were too polite to express our horror and silently shelled out $7.50 each for the ordeal. Alvira then wanted to paint our fingernails and toenails, but we begged off and fled.

It took many weeks to get the coloring out of our hair. We tried everything, including Ajax cleanser. And it was months before it grew back to decent lengths. We were not in good humor during that time. Nor were we great advertisements for Miss Alvira's business.

As a result of our unfortunate experiences, only a few Muckluck women dared put themselves in Miss Alvira's hands. And those who did never went back for seconds.

Wilma Moffid braved a facial, complaining that her skin had become very dry after two pregnancies. However, the facial caused red blotches to appear on Wilma's pretty face. Thankfully, they faded with time, but the eyebrow plucking left her looking perpetually startled. Those little "treats" set her back $5.75, as I recall, and from then on Wilma had to pencil on her eyebrows in order to look normal.

Violet Carson had her nails trimmed, shaped and painted bright red. They looked pretty for a few days, but then the polish started to chip and peel. Violet felt she had wasted a buck-fifty. Benny said he preferred the natural look to the "bloody red claws" anyway.

Miss Alvira stuck it out for a few months, and then one day she was gone. Shortly thereafter, a truck arrived from Seward. Two brawny men jumped out, loaded up the equipment, and Miss Elvira's Emporium Of Beauty was no more. They even took the sign. The building stayed bright pink until another business came to town. Mercifully, the new owner repainted it.

We took a lot of kidding about our new looks, but what the heck, we were used to being the butt of jokes. Even Olav just had to get his two cents worth in.

"I suppose if Miss Alvira had offered to give you a face lift, you'd have gone for that, too," he said, and then winked wickedly.

I think I wrote a poem about a face lift. I wrote it years after I left Muckluck. Let me dig around here for a minute and maybe I can find it.

Yup, here it is. Maybe you'll take a lesson from it.

Saving Face

My friend just had a facelift.
It wasn't necessary.
I thought she looked quite lovely
But she felt old and scary.

It's true, she had some laugh lines
Hugging loosely round her mouth.
And underneath her jaw line
The skin was heading south.

Soft webs fanned out around her eyes
That always shone so bright.
The little satchels 'neath each eye
On her looked somehow right.

But Lulu was unhappy with
The image that she saw.
She didn't like the changes
That time began to draw.

And so she went beneath the knife
In a surgeon's eager hands.
He sliced and diced each blemish;
Stretched her skin like rubber bands.

She spent a fortune on this face
(I shudder at the cost)
For though she does look younger
Something priceless has been lost.

The sands of time had sculpted
The story of her life
And left a soft memorial
Of happiness and strife.

Without those lines and wrinkles
Lulu's essence now has flown.
She appears a smooth, blank stranger
Whom I have never known.

I admit I'm somewhat jealous
When I see her new formed face,
But I'll try to age as Mama did —
With wrinkles AND with grace.

~ 28 ~

Another business that seemed like a good idea at the time came to us in the person of Ashvin Ramaiah. The East Indian gentleman appeared one day riding shotgun in Izzy's freight and mail truck.

Mr. Ramaiah created a bit of a stir as he stepped delicately out of the truck in front of the post office, wearing little cloth shoes and a three-quarter length "jacket" over skin-tight leggings. All pristine white. His head was bald as a bullet, but he sported a full moustache and wire-rim glasses. His skin was as brown as a Hershey chocolate bar.

Ashvin, for that's what we called him since none of us could pronounce his last name, spoke precise English with a charming East Indian accent. He was all smiles and very polite as he inquired of Molly if she knew a place where he could house his business.

"What kind of business?" Molly wanted to know.

Why he was both a yoga master and a psychic, he said.

Molly told him about the building recently vacated by Miss Alvira. Ashvin immediately moved in. His business didn't require complicated equipment like the Emporium of Beauty. In fact, it didn't require anything at all, except a dozen tightly rolled grass mats and some candles. Ashvin was his own equipment.

The evening of his arrival, Chez Buffet hosted him. Word spread quickly around town, and nearly everyone wanted to meet our exotic new citizen and learn more about him and his business.

Ashvin was happy to oblige. In a soft, sing-song voice, he explained some of the mental, physical and spiritual disciplines of yoga, which originated in ancient India.

While not going into great detail, he promised that the practice of yoga would greatly enhance one's spiritual and mental tranquility, while improving one's physical dexterity, energy and strength.

That sounded real good to us, even if we didn't understand it by half. We were sure we could use all of that, though.

Carol, Granny Annie, myself and several others "signed up" for lessons. They were scheduled to be held every Monday and Thursday and would cost one dollar each. It seemed a little steep, but with all the good stuff he promised, we figured it would be well worth the price.

Even more than the yoga, though, we were interested in Ashvin's other specialty. He was, after all, a psychic medium.

About this, he was more mysterious. He only said that since the age of five, when he was trampled by a white water buffalo while playing in the streets of Calcutta, he had been blessed with the ability to not only foresee the future, but to speak with the dead.

He did not read Tarot cards, nor did he gaze into a crystal ball. He did not hear voices, either. He simply sat with his client on the grass mats and meditated until a message came through. These "readings" were one dollar each, also.

That sounded like more fun than yoga. So once again, Carol and I were first in line. We just couldn't help ourselves.

Ashvin began making appointments for about twenty people on his calendar. Nearly all of them were women, but one or two men showed an interest, too.

Ashvin lightened the bright, pink paint on his building. It became less flashy and softer. He said it gave off happy energy. He also painted one of the interior walls a soft, periwinkle blue. It was against that wall that he sat in the lotus position while conducting yoga or psychic readings. His clients sat on mats facing him and the peaceful blue wall.

Yoga sessions were conducted in groups, but the psychic readings were strictly private. We began our journey to higher consciousness with our first yoga lesson.

Ashvin had covered the only window in the room with a large piece of tarpaper left over from Alvira's reconstruction. The room was lit with a few candles, as Carol and I, along with six other women and one man, unrolled mats and sat facing Ashvin. The room smelled exotically of patchouli and curry — though I didn't know anything about those things then. Ashvin explained more about the disciplines of yoga and warned us not to push too hard.

"Be kind to your body and it will be kind to you," he said. Ashvin promised an enlightenment of our higher consciousness, or words to that effect.

The first pose was the downward dog posture. Ashvin demonstrated, and we attempted to mimic him. We put our faces and feet flat on our mats and pointed our hind ends toward the ceiling. Not the most graceful picture, but we were all in the same boat and tried not to giggle.

Next came the bow. A little harder. You lie on your stomach, bend your legs at the knees, lift your torso up and grasp your ankles. Not as easy as the dog.

We moved on to wheel and crane and cobra. By the time we made it to fetus and cow face, I thought I would die. And afraid I wouldn't.

Ashvin would hum softly from time to time — a one-note drone that would have been hypnotic, if we hadn't been in so much pain. At last the session was over.

Our instructor told us to lie on our backs, relax completely from the roots of our hair to the very tips of our toes. Then breathe in gently through our noses and expel the bad air from our mouths.

At that point I was panting so hard, I didn't care where the air was coming from or where it went. Carol flopped limply on the mat next to mine, sweating and moaning softly.

We finally stood, faced Ashvin and placed our palms together. At his command, we murmured "Namaste," which is a form of greeting or farewell, roughly meaning "I bow to you."

Ashvin smiled broadly, collected his fee from each of us and we staggered out the door. We were due back in three days.

The following day I could barely get out of bed. I ached all over, from "the roots of my hair to the tips of my toes."

Carol made it to my place late in the afternoon. She looked like she'd been mauled by a bear. She was in such pain that she couldn't lift her arms to brush her teeth or hair.

We concluded that we had not listened to our bodies, and our bodies were screaming at us now.

"Don't ever do that again!" our bodies were yelling.

In an effort to be fair, we decided we had simply pushed too hard. We should have done the positions more gently and not tried to compete with Ashvin and the others.

So we drank coffee and swallowed three aspirins each. By evening, we felt well enough to heat up some soup for supper. Both of us were moving slowly, but at least we were mobile.

While neither of us ever wanted to attempt a dog or cow or fetus pose again, we also didn't want to hurt Ashvin's feelings. More importantly, we wanted to test his psychic abilities. Our plan was to keep our "reading appointments" the next night and then conveniently come down with the flu to avoid future yoga lessons.

As it happened, we weren't the only ones suffering and plotting how to skip the yoga classes. On Thursday, only two people showed up — and that was their last lesson. I apologize to all true practitioners of yoga. They seem to get real benefit from it. As for me, I'll only say "yoga is a lot harder than it looks!" Namaste to you.

But I digress. All the next day, Carol and I eagerly awaited our upcoming psychic readings. After dinner at Carol's, we walked over to Ashvin's place, which now bore a skinny, plywood sign.

YOGA LESSONS AND PSYCHIC READINGS HEREIN

I hung around outside while Carol had her reading. It took only about twenty minutes, and then it was my turn.

When I walked inside, I noticed the room looked much as it had during the yoga session, except this time there was only one candle struggling against the darkness. Again Ashvin sat in the lotus pose, head bowed, in deep meditation.

I took off my shoes and sat gingerly on the mat in front of him. All was silent for several minutes. Ashvin breathed deeply, until I feared he had fallen asleep. But no, suddenly from his mouth came a deep, familiar voice. It sounded like my father.

"Pug," the voice said. "Look in the bird book."

"Daddy, is that you?" I asked nervously.

The voice certainly sounded like Daddy's, and he had called me Pug because of my short, pugged nose when I was a kid.

"Yesssssss, it's me, Pug. Look in the bird book."

"Okay, Daddy, I'll do it. Where are you and what's it like over there?" I had a million questions, but I went blank at that moment. "Is Ma with you?"

"Yessssss, Ma is here. She wants to talk to you, but it's my turn this time. It's beautiful here. We're very happy. I can't stay, but when you come again, Ma will tell you all about it."

And he was gone, just like that.

Ashvin shuddered a few times, cleared his throat, and held out his hand for his dollar. I really expected more for my buck, but it was clear to me that my time was up.

Carol and I spent the evening at her place talking about our readings. Carol's had been a little longer than mine. She told me all about it.

Although she'd been eager to speak with her dead husband, he never showed up. A little girl spoke briefly. Something about butterflies, but that made no sense at all to Carol.

Then suddenly Ashvin sneezed three times.

"There is a woman," he told Carol. "She is carrying something large and heavy. She talks very softly, but says 'I see you and your friend. Thank you for the flowers.' Now she is gone. Oh, here comes the little girl again. She is holding the woman's hand and they are walking to the creek."

Carol said she was taken aback. She was sure it was the washer woman I told you about before. Was the little girl Sadie Eades?

"Hey, is that you, Sadie?" Carol wanted to know. Ashvin's hand moved in a "be quiet" way, and Carol shut up.

"I see a man in your future," Ashvin continued. "He is younger than you, but you will find love with him. You will travel far from here to be with him. I cannot see his name, but I see the letter X. That is all for this reading."

He took Carol's dollar and blew out the candle. Carol made her way to the door where I waited.

Well, I felt cheated. All I got was a voice that may or may not have been my father's. Oh yeah, he did tell me to look in the "bird book."

I had to think a while before I told Carol that among my family's collection there was a book of John James Audubon's bird paintings. That must be what he was talking about. I said I'd check when I got home, but frankly, was disappointed.

Carol had more to say. She was seriously spooked about the woman and little girl. The fact that the woman had mentioned us bringing her flowers was especially chilling.

Then I suddenly remembered the dress little Sadie was wearing when she drowned. It was yellow with a purple butterfly print on the skirt. Our eyes bugged, and we rubbed the goose pimples on our arms. To say we were freaked out, as the kids today say, would be an understatement.

Then came the prediction about Carol finding love with a younger man. Carol sniffed and looked wryly at me.

"I seriously doubt that's going to happen," she scoffed. "There's no man around here I'd even let kiss me!"

"I know," I argued, "but he said you'd travel far to be with him, so maybe you will be lucky and find love again."

We batted that idea back and forth for a while, until the coffee pot was empty. Then it was time for me to leave.

After I got home, lit my lamp and stoked up the fire, I looked through the shelves where I kept my books. The Audubon book was not hard to find, as it was taller and wider than most of the books.

I took it carefully from the shelf and sat down at the table before I opened it. The book hadn't been opened in years. In fact,

I didn't remember seeing it since I was a little girl. I remembered Daddy looking at the pictures and reading some of the text to me when I was about six or so, but that's all.

As I slowly turned the pages, memories came flooding back. I could almost see Ma over by the cook stove, stirring something in a big, black pot. I strained to hear my brother and sister laughing as they played a game of Chinese checkers on the floor by the wood stove.

I remembered sitting on Daddy's lap and the scent of his plaid, wool shirt. And the prickly way his whiskers felt as he gently rubbed them across my cheek. I could see his big, calloused hands turn the pages carefully, almost reverently, as he read the captions beneath the pictures. He read poorly, for he had very little education, but his joy at the beautiful prints was catching. I'd clap my hands as we marveled at the bright plumage and odd beaks on some of the birds. We had laughed together at some of the stranger looking fine-feathered friends.

In a flash, I came back to earth, landing with a thud. I'd just turned the page that showed a bright, pink flamingo standing on one leg in a pool of water. On the next page there was an envelope.

I removed the envelope and saw the flap was not sealed. I peeked inside. I couldn't believe my eyes. I pulled out five twenty dollar bills — one hundred dollars! A small fortune in those days, especially in Muckluck.

This was Daddy's stash. He had been saving change from his paychecks for years, apparently cashing it in at the store when he had twenty dollars' worth. He'd always told us kids to "save for a rainy day," and this was Daddy's rainy day fund. He died before he could tell Ma about it, and now it was mine. I still couldn't believe it, but undoubtedly, Daddy's message had come through Ashvin. There was no other explanation.

As late as it was, I ran back to Carol's cabin, holding the bills tightly in my hand. When she heard the story, she was as flabbergasted as I. It was early the next morning before I got to bed and fell asleep, the bills still clutched in my hand.

I contacted my brother and sister and told them of my find. But I didn't mention Ashvin's role in it. They would think it was just too weird. Both were happy for me, but said they were doing well and that I should keep the money.

"After all," brother Ted said, "you're keeping up the old home place, and you deserve it."

I was tickled to accept their generosity. I sure could use the money.

We had to wait several years before Carol's prophesy came true. I'm getting a little ahead of myself here, but I'll tell you that Carol did meet and fall in love with a man on a visit Outside to see her children. His name was Xavier Cruz, and although he was ten years younger than Carol, they married and were very happy.

Getting back to Ashvin's business. It didn't take long before he lost all his yoga clients. We were either too old, too banged up physically or too tightfisted to spend money just to cause our bodies more pain. However, he did very well with his psychic readings.

Bob Dodson tramped all over the country trying to locate a moose for his family's winter meat supply that fall. After an unsuccessful week, a disgusted, bush-weary Bob made an appointment with Ashvin. I don't know who "came through" with the hunting information, but Bob was told he needed to look just a little farther southwest of where he had been searching.

Bob did as he was told, and in no time bagged a bull moose that dressed out at nearly seven hundred pounds. Bob became a real fan of psychic readings.

When young Esther Shuler lost the necklace her boyfriend gave her for her birthday, she was heartbroken. Ashvin — or one of Esther's deceased relatives — came through and told her to look under the wooden steps leading to the store. Sure enough, there was the trinket.

So everything was looking rosy for Ashvin. His "gift" was providing a comfortable living, a little nest egg, and grateful clients also brought him gifts of food.

After a successful "reading," during which his dead mother came through with two of her secret gourmet recipes, Chef Buffet gave Ashvin free meals for a month. And we all enjoyed the new menu items.

Then one day Mrs. Eversall's old cow came wondering into town. Ashvin just happened to be looking out his window and caught sight of the cow, a sacred figure to his people. He raced to embrace her with religious fervor.

Old Bossy was practically blind, but when she made out a little figure in white dashing toward her with arms outstretched, she put down her head and butted him right on his bald, brown noggin. Knocked him arse over teakettle and out cold as a mackerel. Granny Annie saw it happen and ran for Carol.

In due time, Ashvin came 'round again, woozy, but otherwise all in one piece. Carol and Mr. Nielson helped him back to his place, where he lay on a mat and stared at the ceiling for almost an hour. Carol thought he might have a concussion, so she watched him carefully, not letting him fall asleep. She kept talking to him and patting his hands and chest, and he finally sat up and smiled dreamily.

Neighbors who gathered were relieved to see their little friend looking and talking quite normal. Carol spent the night watching Ashvin closely, and he seemed to be fine.

But he wasn't fine. The next time a client came for a reading, absolutely nothing happened. Nobody "came through." No messages from the beyond. No predictions of things to come. Nothing. Ashvin had lost his gift just as quickly as it had come to him so many years earlier.

It was a great loss for Ashvin. And for the Muckluckers. Although we never did understand his "gift," we appreciated the help he had so generously given us. He hung around town for a couple of weeks, but sadly decided he would return to India and his family. We gave him a first-class send-off, with many hugs and a few tears. We predicted we would never forget Ashvin Ramaiah and his friends from the other side.

~ 29 ~

I think I've forgotten to mention one of Muckluck's most interesting and beloved citizens. Now how in the world could I do that? I must be slippin'!

I don't recall exactly when she arrived, but I think it was soon after Chef Buffet hired and fired the two "ladies of the evening." She rode over with Reverend Sneed one day and never left. Oh, I remember the day she came to Muckluck so clear.

It had been raining for two weeks straight, and we were all sick and tired of it. So when a sunny, spring day finally arrived, I enjoyed it outdoors, planting nasturtium seeds in a big, old, wooden half barrel.

I love nasturtiums — especially when you bite the tips off their tiny tails and suck the nectar out. Or when you add them to some fresh spinach with a few raisins for a colorful and healthy salad. Drizzle some vinegar and oil over 'em. Yum, yum! I wish I had a mess of them right now.

But I'm wandering again. Get back to your story, Kate.

As I looked up from my task, I saw the Reverend's car pull up in front of the store. A tall lady climbed out.

She was dressed stylishly in a royal blue, flowered dress, and she wore a matching hat on top of her brown curls. The lady saw me staring. She carefully picked her way around mud puddles in her ivory-colored high heels and then offered her hand.

"Why hello! I am Elly Kay Ott," she said, in a low, musical voice. "Pleased to make your acquaintance."

I wiped my dirty hands on my jeans a few times before I dared take her white-gloved hand. For a large-boned lady, her shake was kind of wimpy, but her smile made up for it. She dazzled.

I introduced myself and invited Elly in for a cup of coffee and a slice of jellyroll I'd made the day before.

She readily accepted. We soon were sitting at my wobbly table, enjoying the snack and each other's company. She didn't say much about herself, except that she came from California and she would like to settle in a "sweet little town like Muckluck."

Elly asked a lot of questions about the town. She wanted to know about its people, the weather and chances of finding work here.

I was pretty up on the answers — except for the job question. There really wasn't much work to be had in Muckluck, unless Martin was hiring at the saw mill. And that was obviously out of the question. I tried to be encouraging, while still being truthful.

After our visit, Elly attended the church service over at the school. Then before the Reverend left for Seward, she lugged two huge suitcases and a hat box out of his car's trunk and stood in the middle of the road, looking around expectantly. It was obvious she planned to stay for a while.

Wilma Moffid saw her standing there. She went over to see if she could be of any help, and after they talked for a while, Wilma picked up the handle of one of the suitcases. Elly grabbed the other suitcase and hat box, and the pair moved off toward Wilma's place. Not surprisingly, Wilma had felt sorry for Elly and invited her to spend the night with her and Dave.

The next morning Elly, dressed to the nines again, set off to inquire about gainful employment. Bing and Val didn't need any help at the store, and Izzy didn't need help on his truck route.

Our two game guides looked doubtfully at Elly's high heels and ruffled frock. Snickering up their sleeves, they didn't see Elly as a game guide or horse wrangler. Hank Hazelton said he could use a hand with his dogs, but he didn't have any money for wages.

Feeling a little discouraged, but with erect posture and a big smile, Elly walked into Chez Buffet and charmed the apron off Armand. It had been a long time since he'd seen such a refined lady, and he was fascinated.

Though she'd never had any waitressing experience, she convinced him she was a fast learner. And to top it off, she was an

162

excellent dessert cook. Armand hired her on the spot and found her a room to rent with Granny Annie.

Business at Chez Buffet picked up immediately. Customers flocked to meet the glamorous lady in her pretty dresses and glittering jewelry. She was an exotic bird come to brighten our drab little nest. Her only concession was to trade her high heels for a pair of tennis shoes. They were so much easier on the feet and back when waiting tables. But I know she hated to part with those high heels.

Elly soon had the admiration of the men, the friendship of the women and the love of the children. In her spare time, she helped Thelma at the school. She came up with artsy-craftsy projects and told fantastic stories in her gentle voice.

The kids were thrilled by her sophistication, and many a little girl wanted to grow up to be "just like Miss Elly." Their mothers were fond of Elly, too.

At their suggestion, Elly held monthly "charm classes." She had an enormous supply of cleansing and wrinkle-removing creams, which she demonstrated on any women wanting to try them. She even let us experiment with her makeup.

She told us not to copy her style, but to find our own beauty and enhance it. In the end, very few of us kept up our "new look," although a few started wearing a touch of lipstick or rouge on special occasions. And our fingernails, although not painted, became less ragged and considerably cleaner.

Another specialty of Elly's was to teach us what colors most complimented our complexions. She'd select one of her pretty frocks and hold it in front of this woman or that. Then she would point out if it was a good color for her, or not. This information, while fun and interesting, didn't "stick" very long with us. We kept wearing what we'd always worn — blue jeans and sweat shirts or flannel plaids in whatever color we happened to own.

Elly did talk some of us out of our ponytails, though, even convincing a few to experiment with Toni Home Perms. Mine was not a raving success.

She let us try on her sparkling costume jewelry, too, and showed us how to walk gracefully, even in sneakers and boots. It was always such fun to get together and see what Elly had for us each month. We shared lots of laughter, some gossip and a glass or two of homemade berry wine. We always learned something new and exciting from Elly.

Those sessions lasted about six months. Then we all, including Elly, grew tired of trying to glamorize Muckluck. We went back to our old ways.

Elly, not a bit discouraged, continued to be her charming self. She was always well groomed in a bright frock and applied just the right amount of cosmetics and sparkle. And she always wore a smile.

In order to continue our happy monthly get-togethers, Elly started a knitting circle. She taught us how to knit caps, mittens and scarves. We knit until we were sick and tired of it.

Then she held cooking classes. We learned to make some fancy desserts and a few Chinese dishes. We couldn't wait for Elly's next grand idea.

In the meantime, Elly continued working at Chez Buffet. After a while, her fetching ways caused Armand's romantic French heart to do odd things whenever she was around. He developed a crush on her.

She tried to kindly discourage him. But as time went by, his ardor only grew stronger. Then one fine day, amid the pots and pans and scraps of food in the restaurant's kitchen, Armand got down on his knee and asked Elly Kay to marry him.

To say she was speechless is an understatement. She fled.

Elly rushed over to my place. And this time, she wasn't smiling. As a matter of fact, she was dabbing at her eyes with a lace-trimmed hanky, clearly distraught.

I warmed up the coffee, and we sat at the table looking searchingly at each other. I've found over the years that the kitchen table and a cup of coffee are the most comforting things to have handy during a serious discussion.

I let Elly take the lead. For a long time she just sat there brushing away tears as they ran down her face, leaving tracks through the rouge, and dripping off her chin.

Finally she began to speak.

"Katie, I've got a confession to make. I'd go to Father Sorinoff, but I don't think he'd understand at all," she said through sniffles. "I wanted to tell Reverend Sneed when we drove here, but I just couldn't find the courage."

"Honey, I'm your friend," I said, and urged her to go on. "I'll understand. Just tell me whatever it is that's bothering you."

And she did. Oh boy, did she ever. Elly Kay Ott was actually Elliott Kaye!

Originally from Kansas, he had served four years in the U.S. Army. He rose to the rank of staff sergeant and was honorably discharged after the war.

Instead of going home to his family farm, he migrated to San Francisco. Elliott didn't know a soul. He was miserably lonesome. Then one evening he found himself in an unusual nightclub. All the customers were men.

Because he had a comely face and nice manners, he soon had many new friends who bought him drinks. He wasn't accustomed to the attention or the drinking.

He said his new friends took advantage of his youth and ignorance. And he soon found himself involved in a lifestyle not to his liking. He hated it.

But he had friends and didn't want to lose them. So he found a way to keep his friends, and yet not take part in their activities.

You see, every night at the club the lights dimmed and gorgeously gowned "ladies" appeared on stage. They sang and danced and told jokes. These "ladies" were actually men.

It's hard to believe, but these men enjoyed dressing up and pretending to be women. And the customers loved their performances. These men were truly queens of the club.

Elliott found that if he became one of the entertainers, he could still be with his friends, but he could discourage their advances.

He explained to his friends that he would rather be a woman and not a homosexual. Because they were good friends, and truly cared about him, they accepted his choice.

So he went to a thrift store and bought the most elaborate dresses and shoes he could find. He also bought makeup and a long, blond wig. He then let his fingernails grow and painted them a flaming red.

Elliott had a nice voice, which he trained to sound softly feminine. He practiced walking in high heels and even learned to dance a little.

When he felt he was ready, he donned his new look and presented himself to the club's owner. He was hired on the spot. He then rearranged the letters in his name and became Elly Kay Ott.

Elly worked at the club for nearly ten years. Elliott's friends remained Elly's friends. They always treated her like a lady and didn't "bother" her.

But as the years went by, Elly became tired of singing and dancing at the club. She still wanted to be a woman, but she wanted a more normal life.

Then she met a man from Alaska one night. He told her Alaska was a place where people accepted you for yourself and didn't ask questions. After giving it a lot of thought, Elly decided Alaska might be a good place to find acceptance — and a home.

She took a bus to Seattle, caught the first steamship out and disembarked in Seward. While she liked Seward, she was afraid someone might recognize her there — perhaps the man who'd told her about Alaska in the first place.

So she asked folks to tell her about nearby towns. That's how she learned about Muckluck. Elly liked what she heard. And when she got there, and met some of the folks, she knew she'd found her home.

Everything had been wonderful. She loved the Muckluckers and they loved her. But now Chef Buffet had fallen in love and wanted to marry her.

Oh my stars — what a predicament. I'd never heard of anything like that. My grandson told me years later that Elly was a transvestite, or a person who liked to wear the clothes of the opposite sex. He explained that it was a psychological urge and that Elly probably couldn't help herself. Well, I didn't know that when she dumped her news on me, so I was at a real disadvantage.

Two things I knew for sure. One, Elly was my friend. Two, she was in deep distress.

"I like and admire Armand so much. He's my best friend and my boss, and I wouldn't want to hurt him for the world," Elly said through gulps of air as she continued sobbing into her now-soaked hanky. "How can I break his heart by refusing his proposal? But how can I tell him my secret?"

We fussed over the problem for several hours. I was still in shock, remembering all the while that I was talking to a man and not a woman.

Elly worried what the rest of the town would think if her secret got out. How would parents feel about her being around their kids? Would people think it was sick or would they snicker and make jokes at her expense? Would Chef Buffet be embarrassed? Would he fire her? What would she do then? She so loved her job and Muckluck.

After we'd consumed enough coffee to float the *Titanic*, we knew we'd have to make a decision. Form a plan, so to speak.

Worn out and limp from crying, Elly couldn't think straight. But she'd trusted me with her story and asked for my help, so I gave her my best advice. I thought she should go to Armand and tell him the whole story, just like she had told it to me.

"Then tell him you will never tell another living soul about his proposal," I said. "If he truly loves you, and is your friend, I think he'll understand. He has a warm heart and he's a good man."

I then told her that I thought we should call a town meeting and explain the situation to all the adults.

"My daddy always said, 'Honesty is the best policy,' and I can't think of any other way to handle this," I said.

I asked her if she could stand in front of the whole town and tell them her story. She'd have to explain that she had no romantic interest in anyone, especially children, and wouldn't in a million years hurt a single soul. I told her I would stand beside her and speak on her behalf.

"I think if we're honest, and you can answer their questions, they'll remember how much they admired and cared about you this past year," I said. "I think they'll accept you just as you are."

Elly wrung out her hanky over my slop bucket again. She looked to be about out of tears. She then grasped my hands in her two big hands, which sported shocking-pink fingernail polish, and looked deep into my eyes.

"Katie, you are a true friend," she said. "I think your solution is the only way to go. It's either that or sneak out of town like a thief — and I don't want to do that."

She said Muckluck deserved better and the good people needed to know all about her.

I walked her home, gave her a tight hug and promised to invite everyone to a town meeting the following evening. That would give her time to handle Chef Buffet first. I wished her luck with that. Then I went back to my cabin and prayed a lot.

To make this long story a bit shorter, I'll only tell you that Elly did confess to Armand. Although he was thoroughly shocked, and sorely disappointed, he understood completely. After all, he was French and knew about all kinds of different human behaviors. They hugged and agreed to remain best friends and co-workers.

Most everybody in Muckluck showed up for the town meeting. I had said it was something important regarding Elly Kay, and everyone was interested in Elly. They came, they heard, and they asked lots of questions. All but one or two gave her a standing ovation, big hugs and the Muckluck seal of approval.

In the end, nothing changed. Elly still worked with the kids at school. She still held classes in arts, crafts and home decorating. She was still admired and loved. In this one case, "she told and we asked." And we were all better people because of it.

A Bodacious Lady

A quaint, bodacious lady
Once lived next door to me.
She had nine cats and thirteen dogs
And an owl in a willow tree.

Vermillion curls hung down her back
And glasses set low on her nose.
On her feet she wore sequined sandals,
While her closet held fabulous clothes.

I once peeked inside of its vastness
And discovered — not to my surprise
A veritable treasure of goodies
That dazzled my nine-year-old eyes.

There were muumuus and caftans and minis,
Net stockings and bright, spangled tights,
Feather boas in purple and aqua
And nighties that lit up the nights.

Some gossamer garments were flimsy,
Diaphanous fabrics so rare
Embellished with pearls and rhinestones
Embroidered with scrupulous care.

Oh, how I admired that lady!
Such glamour I'd not ever seen.
I tried to mimic her grandness
For she was my fabulous queen.

I thought she was fantastic!
And I knew one thing for sure:
When I grew up I planned to be
Bodacious — just like her!

~ 30 ~

Now that I think about it, there was another person in Muckluck you should meet. He lived there all his life. In fact, he was such a familiar figure around town that we forgot that he was different. He was black.

Leviticus Jones was the only black person in town. Maybe on the whole Kenai Peninsula for all I know. We had some light-brown people, some dark-brown people, and lots of white and pink people. Nanny Burrows, for instance, with her rosy-colored hair and freckles all over, actually looked more pink than anything.

But Leviticus was black like the Africans on the pages of *National Geographic*. While it didn't matter to Muckluckers what color you were, I have to admit that Leviticus stood out in a crowd. He was the tallest person in town and had huge hands and feet. He sported wooly, black hair, and his teeth, against that black skin, were as white as new-fallen snow.

He once told me that his great-grandfather had been a slave in Alabama and was freed following the Emancipation Proclamation of 1863. He became a farmer on a small piece of land given him by his former "master," who must have considered him special. He married another freed slave. They grew cotton, raised a family and did pretty well for themselves.

Leviticus was proud of the way his ancestors had survived and prospered after living in the awful conditions of slavery. His grandpa, son of the cotton farmer, became a merchant. He sold this and that to other black folks and was highly respected in and around Autauga County.

During the gold rush of the early 1900s, Leviticus' father set off to find his fortune in Alaska. Unlike most, he brought his wife along. What a hard life they must have led. Like most, they didn't find the gold, but they were among the early settlers of Muckluck.

Leviticus was born about the same time as me. His mother wanted to give him a good, strong, Bible name. When we kids tried to call him Levi for short, he always corrected us.

"My name is Leviticus, now and evermore!" he'd proudly say. And so it was.

We grew up together and were great friends. Some of the kids liked to touch his hair and pet his skin, but Leviticus didn't mind. I think he enjoyed being different. He was athletic and ready for adventure, so he was always the leader in our games and ramblings.

He was a little old when World War II broke out, but he joined up anyway. The Army gratefully accepted him. When the fighting ended, he came home to Muckluck. His hair showed sprinkles of white, and his face was a lot sadder.

But that wonderful, toothy, white smile still lit his face. Especially when kids were around. It became his great pleasure to help out at the school, teaching the kids to read music and leading them in song.

His specialty was songs that tickled the kids' funny bones, including "Mares Eat Oats and Does Eat Oats," "Three Little Fishes" and "Chickery Chick Cha-la Cha-la." He also loved old-time spirituals like "Swing Low Sweet Chariot," "Oh Them Golden Slippers," and revival hymns like "Beulah Land."

While his rich, tenor voice rang out joyfully, Leviticus waved his arms and kept time pounding his big foot on the floor. The old schoolhouse jumped when Leviticus led the singing.

He never had a girlfriend that we knew of. Maybe he had a romance or two when he was overseas, but never in Muckluck. Then when the highway between Seward and Anchorage was completed around 1951, we had a lot more company and more changes to meet other people.

The traffic went both ways — especially on weekends. While Muckluckers craved the change of pace and scenery offered by the "big city," folks from Anchorage liked to come and enjoy the quaintness of our little town.

Usually it was a friendly exchange, but sometimes there were problems.

Hard liquor was sometimes brought in, and once in a while a fight would break out. But things still were pretty mellow in Muckluck.

Leviticus bought an old Chevy sedan that he loved like a brother. He tinkered with it until it purred like a kitten. He kept it spotless, despite rain, hail, snow or mud. Though gasoline was in short supply, he still made trips to Seward and Anchorage as often as he could. On one such trip he met a young lady named Pearl. He was bit by the Love Bug at first sight.

Pearl worked as a nurse's aide at the hospital in Anchorage. She was as ebony as Leviticus and breathtakingly beautiful.

When the hometown boy brought her back to Muckluck, we were blown over by what a striking couple they made. And sing? Oh my stars and bars, when those two sang together, it was like listening to angels.

Leviticus wanted to ask for Pearl's hand in marriage. I know that to be a fact because he showed me a diamond ring that had belonged to his mother. The stone was small, but it shone like a star. And it was set in pure Alaska gold. It may have been made from the only gold Leviticus' father ever found. He, like most Muckluckers, did not have much luck mucking.

My friend planned to pop the question on his next trip to the city. But it was winter, and he was waiting until the highway was cleared of new snow.

As it almost always happens, disaster struck without warning. Olav got a message from the Anchorage Police that Pearl Johnson was dead. She had listed Leviticus as her contact person on forms at the hospital.

It seems Pearl and some friends were skating at Sand Lake, where snow had been cleared from the ice to make a nice area for young people to skate. We knew Pearl was a good skater. I saw her skate when she came to Muckluck, and she was by far the best I've ever seen.

So it was an awful shock to learn that she'd tripped over a twig frozen in the ice, fell and hit her head — hard. She was taken to the very hospital where she worked, so I know they did their best for her. But she had bleeding on her brain and died shortly after getting there. She never did regain consciousness.

Olav brought the message to me, so we could go together to break the horrible news to Leviticus. Oh, you'll never know how bad I hated to do it. He was sitting in his cabin, writing something on a yellow tablet. We heard him singing softly as we stood outside his door.

At our knock, he stopped singing. His chair scraped shrilly as he pushed away from the table. Olav grabbed my hand for courage as the door opened, and there was Leviticus' smiling face.

It was one of the hardest things I've ever had to do.

Leviticus just crumbled at the news. His knees gave way and he sank to the floor with his hands over his face. He just moaned and rocked from side to side. Olav and I knelt on either side of him, put our arms around him and we all cried. Even Olav.

Later that day, Leviticus showed me what he was writing when we brought him the terrible news. It was a love poem for Pearl. He wasn't happy with it and asked me for help. I did my best and then made copies for Leviticus and me to keep.

I learned that Pearl was buried with the original in her hand.

My Pearl

A Pearl of wisdom, I submit
Is much to be admired.
For Pearls of wisdom are so rare
And much to be desired.

"Cast not your Pearls before the swine"
For they know not the worth
Of precious Pearls, so rarely found
Upon this troubled earth.

A lovely Pearl is softer than
All other gems so bright.
A Pearl does cleverly absorb
As well as reflect light.

God must have loved the Pearl because
He chose for his estate
A luminescent, open door
Within a Pearly gate.

And so I write these words for you
But they do not suffice
To tell you how I treasure you:
My Pearl of great price.

~ 31 ~

Oh, those precious memories. There are so many whirling 'round in my brain, but I don't want to bore you. Aw heck, I'll give you one or two more anyway.

It makes me chuckle to this day to recall the time a traveling salesman came to town. Now his name I don't remember. We just ever after called him Slick. It suited him to a T.

It was in the fall of the year, the leaves turning red, orange and yellow. Days were getting nippier with less daylight, and the geese were beginning to fly south for the winter. Folks were hunkering down again, gearing up for a long, dark spell.

We all knew we would probably have an epidemic of flu and colds in the not-too-distant future. Seems like we always caught the "bugs" every winter. Though how they survived in such weather, I'll never know. Maybe the viruses took up residence in our bodies just to stay warm.

Anyway, one day a fella pulled up in his big, gray Buick. He parked at the store, hopped out and climbed the stairs to the door. Bing and Val, both behind the counter, gave him the usual warm Muckluck welcome and asked if they could help him.

"No sir, no ma'am," he said. "I ain't here to buy nothing. I'm here to sell you something. And when you hear what it is, you are gonna want some just for yourselves and your customers."

He went on to tell them that he was sure they were going to want to invite all their neighbors over for some cookies and coffee and to hear what he had brought in his car.

"We will tell them about my product and they will clean me out," he said. "I've got a trunk full of product, but by the time I leave, I will have one big, empty trunk."

Well now, that got their attention. Val asked just what it was he was selling. He looked slyly around the store, saw that nobody

175

was listening — the old-timers were laughing and visiting over by the stove.

"I'm going to sell you the means to a happy, healthy winter," he whispered. "Are you interested?"

Well, Val had already had that experience with tuberculosis, so she was interested in anything that promised to bring good health.

"What is it?" she wanted to know.

The salesman proudly declared that he had cases of doctor-invented and doctor-recommended Multi-Everwell Liquid.

"It was invented in England by the famous Doctor Haversham and has only recently arrived on our fair shores," he said. "It's a miracle in a bottle!"

So far Bing hadn't said anything, but he finally stepped forward.

"How do we know it brings 'happiness and good health' like you said?" Bing asked.

"Why, from all the letters of praise and gratitude I've got right here," the salesman said, and then waved sheets of paper under their noses. "These folks have had the privilege and pleasure of using Multi-Everwell Liquid, and they ain't ashamed to tell their stories. Here, read a couple."

He pushed the papers at Val. She told me later the letters were full of praise for the product and highly recommended that the reader purchase the product and use as directed.

Bing was not easily hornswoggled, but eventually came 'round.

"Tell you what," Bing said. "I'll take a bottle now, and Val and I'll try it out. If we think it's on the level, we'll invite some folks over and you can give them your spiel. How's that sound?"

Slick said that was fine with him. He'd hang around for a few days, maybe fish for a bit, and await their verdict.

From his deep coat pocket he pulled out a pint-size bottle that contained a yellow-colored liquid. He handed it to Bing.

"This one's on me. For your cooperation," he said. "I know you'll endorse my product. And you'll be a hero for keeping your fair city healthy this winter."

So Val and Bing sampled the bottle that evening. They found it was not unpleasant, although it did have an odd, slightly bitter taste. They each took several good swigs that went down pretty smooth. And both slept like hibernating bears that night.

Val saw Slick talking to some folks across the road from the store the next day. She told Bing, who then walked on over to the salesman and asked if they could try another bottle. One sample didn't seem a fair test of the product.

"Sure, help yourself," Slick said.

So Bing took another bottle from the stash in the back seat of the Buick. He knew there was plenty more in the trunk.

That night they slept very well again, and woke up the next morning feeling rested and full of energy. They decided they would heartily endorse Multi-Everwell Liquid, although they couldn't guarantee it would keep the flu and colds away. That remained to be seen.

That evening they invited a bunch of Muckluckers to the store, where they were treated to the full blast of Slick's enthusiastic sales pitch, along with cookies and coffee.

Slick promised that half a bottle per person would relax and refresh them 'til they felt like newborn babes. If they took the other half the next evening, there would be enough product circulating their systems to protect them from viruses for the rest of the winter. It might even prevent chilblains — and in several cases he could site — hemorrhoids!

"Just one bottle per person will probably do the trick," Slick said. "But two bottles would be even better."

There were lots of questions asked and answered. Slick had answers for every objection.

Now Muckluckers were not sophisticated folks, but they hadn't just fallen off the turnip truck, either. Some were doubtful, but many were interested in this new medical breakthrough.

The cost was steep. Five dollars per bottle. But many Muckluckers thought no price was too high if it kept you flu-and-cold free all winter.

Slick said Multi-Everwell Liquid was selling like hotcakes in England at twice that price, but he was a humanitarian and only wanted to make his costs, with a little profit for living expenses.

Quite a few folks stepped up waving five-dollar bills and happily making their investment in good health. And sure enough, by the time the evening was over, Slick's Buick did not have one single bottle of product left.

The Muckluckers who drank their half bottle that night slept the sleep of the innocent and felt good the next morning. Some of them came over to Izzy's place, where Slick was bunking, to thank him. But Slick was gone. He had to leave real early, he told Izzy on the way out, because he needed to get more product in Seward. And off he went, a happier, richer man.

We all sat back and waited to see if we'd have a healthier winter. But it wasn't long before we learned the truth about the "miracle medicine."

A few weeks after Slick's visit, *The Seward Weekly Gateway* arrived with the mail. That's when we saw the newspaper article.

Seems some folks in Fairbanks got suspicious when Slick was selling his product there. They sent a sample to a laboratory in Oregon, where it was analyzed. The only ingredients in the concoction were unsweetened lemon Kool-Aid and pulverized sleeping pills.

Didn't we feel stupid! Of course the Muckluckers who bought it slept well. And because they slept well, they felt terrific.

We were annoyed as all get-out. Not so much at Slick, but at ourselves for being such fools. We did learn a couple lessons though. Don't be so dang gullible, and check things out thoroughly before you lay down your hard-earned money.

I'd like to think you won't find any moss growing on old Kate's brain since Slick's visit — and I'm not ashamed to admit I'm tight with a dollar. Especially when it comes to spending on "miracles."

And that reminds me of a poem I wrote a couple of years ago. You might enjoy it. Maybe it'll shed light on what the future has in store for you.

Medicine Chest Alphabet

A is for Aspirin, good for my head
I take one each night as I hop into bed.
B is for Band-Aid, to put on an ouch
I boo-booed my finger while moving the couch.
C is for calcium, keeps bones looking smart.
D's digitalis that jump-starts the heart.
E — lovely vitamin — helps us look young.
F is for fish oil, so slick on the tongue.
G is for Geritol, kind to the gut.
H Preparation's for pains in the butt.
I stands for Iodine, careful, don't spill.
J is for jars of creams, crammed to the fill.
K is the Kleenex that catches the sneeze.
L is the lineament rubbed on the knees.
M is Murine that takes out the red.
N is for Nytol that puts me to bed.
O stands for ointment for chapped and dry skin.
P stands for pills and the kind Premarin.
Q is for Q-tips to keep the ears clean.
R — Robitussin for coughs loud and mean.
S is for Sudafed, helps me to nap.
T stands for Tums, reflex acid to zap.
U is for Unguentine — gooey old blend.
V is Viagra, the lover-man's friend.
W is water to wash down the pills.
X are the X-rays that pinpoint my ills.
Y is for youth that has flown out the door.
Z is for zzzzzz — getting old is a snore.

~ 32 ~

It seems to me I've failed to tell you about our animal citizens. Some of them were just as interesting as the two-legged creatures of our town. And some were more interesting and more loved, too.

Sue Martin, out at the saw mill, had a calico cat that she was just crazy about. That cat followed her everywhere she went. In the winter, the cat didn't take to snow on the ground at all. So Sue carried her in a big, green handbag when she came to town. The cat was named, as I recall, Whiskers.

Whiskers was definately a house cat. She didn't hunt for mice, nor did she bring dead birds as gifts for her mistress. Basically, she just lounged around as close to the fireplace as she could get, drank canned milk diluted with water and ate regular people food, which was carefully shredded and minced.

She meowed so loudly during storms that she had to cuddle in bed between Sue and her husband, Harold. That made Whiskers happy, but it didn't help Harold's frame of mind or his romantic efforts. It especially annoyed him when Whiskers crawled up in the middle of the night and flopped directly on Harold's head. Sue insisted on comforting Whiskers during storms, and Harold loved Sue. So there you have it.

Sue brought Whiskers to town one day to do some grocery shopping. It wasn't winter, and there was no snow on the ground. Sue just thought Whiskers would enjoy the outing. She placed her handbag, containing the cat, on the floor of the store while she consulted with Bing about the rising cost of canned peaches.

When Mack and Earl Raben came in to buy some ammo, they accidently left the door open a tad. Whiskers saw her chance and grabbed it. She darted out the door into the street. Tail high and prancing along like a pony, she headed over to the post office.

It just so happened Izzy was there, picking up some outgoing mail to take to Seward. Whiskers jumped into the back of Izzy's truck and snuggled down among the mail sacks. She went to sleep and slept soundly until Izzy stopped the truck in Seward.

Izzy didn't notice when Whiskers leapt down and scooted off to explore her new surroundings. He just picked up the incoming mail and headed back to Muckluck.

When Sue noticed Whiskers had escaped her bag, she flew into a tizzy. She had everyone in town searching for that dang cat. After a few days, Sue resigned herself to the fact that Whiskers was not going to be found.

Harold offered to get her another cat, but she wasn't having any of that. She wallowed in her misery until Harold, although secretly a little pleased not to have to compete with the pesky cat, was at his wits' end. The atmosphere at the saw mill was not a happy one.

Five weeks went by. Then one day Sue looked out her kitchen window and saw Whiskers, limping along, her tail dragging in the dust.

You are not going to believe this, but Whiskers had somehow walked over fifty miles back to her home in Muckluck. She was as skinny as a pencil and the pads of her paws were raw and bloody. But with Sue's tender nursing, lots of shredded chicken meat and bowls of milk, Whiskers soon was back to normal, queen of the house and making Harold miserable.

Then we had some real cute pups around Muckluck, too. You may remember Hank Hazelton, who gave dogsled rides to the kids at the Mid-Winter Madness Festival. Well, every couple of years he'd breed one of his females and have a litter of the cutest little pups you ever saw in your life. When they were weaned, he'd sell them for a real good price.

But one little fella got away. Somehow he wandered off into the woods and just disappeared. Hank felt awful about it and searched for days. He found no sign of the pooch. Then one day he raised his binoculars and searched the side of a mountain.

He saw the craziest darn thing. There was a mama bear with two cubs and Hank's pup! The cubs and the pup were wrestling and rolling around, having the time of their young lives.

Then mama bear lumbered over and gave the signal it was time to move on. Up the mountain they climbed, out of sight in no time.

Hank was floored. He went back to that spot several times, hoping to see the bear family and their adopted son again, but he never did. Until one day about a year later.

He happened to be setting some rabbit traps when he sensed that he was being watched. Hank carefully turned around, and there, not more than a hundred yards away, was a female bear and a gorgeous young dog. Although her other kids had left their old ma, the dog chose to stay with her.

The bear stood on her hind legs and sniffed the air. And I swear, Hank told me honest and true, that dog stood on his hind legs and sniffed, too.

Bears have poor eyesight, but they have a keen sense of smell. Apparently both the bear and the dog were satisfied Hank meant them no harm, for they settled back down and continued on their way. An odd couple indeed, but seemingly a happy one. Hank never saw them again.

It's true that sometimes animals take a strong attachment to creatures not of their own kind. For instance, there was the baby moose a fella over in Hope found. Nearby was the dead mother moose. He couldn't tell what had killed her, or maybe it was just her time to go.

Anyway, he carried the little guy home and raised him. Fed him from a baby bottle until he was old enough to eat naturally.

That Hope man knew he shouldn't keep the young moose around too long or it wouldn't be able to fend for itself in the wilderness. So one day he took him out and left him there, way out in the woods. It was a hard thing to do, but it was the right thing to do.

Well, that moose roamed around the woods, and when his belly started to rumble, he figured he'd better try a nibble of this and that. I know what moose eat, so I imagine he sampled twigs, leaves, lichen and willow branches. And any other vegetation he could find, until he was satisfied. How a moose can survive and grow to such a huge size by eating only "salad" is beyond me.

One day, a year or so later, the moose found himself at Mrs. Eversall's homestead. He meandered over to the corral and spotted old Bossy. Maybe it was love at first sight, lust, or perhaps he thought she was his mother, but that moose fell hard for Bossy.

He hung around, his giant head resting on the fence, mooning over the cow. Every morning when Mrs. Eversall would go out to throw some feed for Bossy, she tossed some over the fence for the moose. In time, Mrs. E grew rather fond of the big beast and named him Galahad.

All was well until Galahad decided he didn't want to be separated from Bossy by the fence. He began ramming it with his antlers.

Mrs. Eversall hurried out and led Bossy into the make-shift barn. When the fence collapsed and Galahad started for the barn, Mrs. Eversall got her gun and shot into the air. Galahad took off, but he was back the next day.

It finally became too much of a trial for Mrs. E. She came to town and asked Olav to contact Bud Reeves, the game warden, and ask him to come and get that moose out of her hair.

Bud got the message and brought the Waldorf twins to help him take care of the problem. After a number of unsuccessful tries, they managed to lasso the moose, and because he had been raised around people, he was really quite tame. They coaxed him into a truck and carted him off to other, hopefully greener, pastures. We all hoped he was never spotted by a hungry hunter. Galahad was a lover, not a fighter.

The next story I want to tell you has to do with chickens and a total eclipse of the sun. Have you ever experienced a total eclipse of the sun?

It's a strange and awesome performance. I remember the day it happened over Muckluck, though I can't recollect the exact year.

I know we were absolutely fascinated to see the previously sunny sky become eerily twilight. Then the sun gradually disappeared as the full moon passed between the earth and the sun, casting its shadow over Muckluck. When the moon was directly in front of the sun, it was surrounded by a filmy halo. And it became dark as night for several minutes.

Nanny Burrows raised chickens in a pen behind her cabin. She'd had Felix build her a nice coop with raised shelves for nests and rails for roosting at night. During the daytime, the chickens enjoyed their little yard, pecking around for a morsel of corn or a bug to snack on.

Nanny was out in her yard watching the eclipse like the rest of us when, as the day grew darker, her chickens lined up, marched into their coop and flew up onto their roosts and went to sleep. Nanny said they looked totally confused when, a few minutes later, the sun came out again, and it was time to "rise and shine." Those chickens must have thought that was the shortest night they'd ever experienced.

Now I wouldn't want you to get the idea that all the animals around Muckluck were as cute, funny, clever and friendly as those I just told you about.

Wild animals have to fend for themselves. They have to find their own food, and they must protect themselves from predators. Since very often wild animals are hunted and killed by humans, you can't blame them for being distrustful and protective when dealing with two-legged critters like us.

I know of three bear attacks that were gosh-awful ugly. In two cases, the men were killed. But in one attack, the victim lived to tell the story.

Phil Vickner was hiking along Moose Run when he suddenly came upon a mother bear and her cubs fishing for spawning salmon. He meant them no harm, but he was too close for mama's comfort.

She galloped toward him faster than you'd think such a big, clumsy-looking animal could move. She was on top of him before he could even turn around. It's probably a good thing he didn't try to run. He fell down in a curled position, covered his head with his arms, hardly daring to breathe.

Mama bear took a couple swipes at him with her long, sharp claws, ripping skin from his back and dislocating one arm. Then she bit him on the shoulder, raked his scalp half off his skull and lumbered away.

Phil lay still as a dead man. He didn't move for five minutes, which he told me felt like five hours. He then cautiously and painfully got up. Bleeding and limping, he made his way back to Muckluck. Carol did her best for him and gave him a shot of morphine. Izzy then drove him to the Seward Hospital, where they did a good job patching him up.

Phil did the right thing. Remember, if you're ever attacked by a grizzly bear, don't try to outrun him or fight him. He doesn't want to eat you, so just lay like a rock and let him have a little fun. He'll soon get tired of you. If you're lucky, you will have a great story to tell your grandchildren.

The other two men ran and fought, and they didn't stand a chance.

Now if you come across a black bear, that's another story. Those fellas are unpredictable. Sometimes you can scare them away, sometimes a swift kick will send them packing. You never know with a blackie.

To be safe, some folks maintain you should talk real loud, sing or jingle "bear bells" when you're walking in the woods. I always felt half the charm of being in the woods was the peace and quiet, so you can enjoy birds singing and the wind whistling through the trees. I don't recommend making loud noises in the woods, but I do recommend you be alert at all times and carry a powerful gun.

Moose are usually pretty calm critters. They more or less mind their own business. After all, they have to spend nearly every waking moment searching for vegetation to eat in order to grow so big and keep up their energy. It takes a lot of strength to lug around those huge antlers.

If you just give a moose his space and leave him alone, he'll usually ignore you. But if you surprise one, or he feels threatened, you'd best watch out. Also keep a lookout for cows with a baby or two. Those mamas are real protective.

When a moose runs out of patience or feels uncomfortable, his ears flatten against the back of his head. Also the hair on his hump stands up stiff, his tongue whips from side to side, and he may even paw at the ground before taking off after you. If you see any of those signs, you'd better run. Chances are, he'll outrun you, but you've gotta give your best effort.

I knew a fellow who was attacked by a big bull moose. I don't know what he did to make the animal so mad, but the moose knocked him down and then proceeded to trample him with his front hooves. The man had half of his ribs broken and was pretty messed up inside, but he survived.

There were two girls walking to school who surprised a moose once, too. They must have scared him 'cause he lowered his head and started after them. They ran, but they could hear him snorting and huffing as he gained on them.

The girls' guardian angel must have been keeping close watch that day, for they both tripped over a big fallen tree and lay cuddled tightly against that log. The moose jumped right over the log and the girls and ran on 'til he was out of sight.

We had mice in Muckluck, too. We set traps baited with peanut butter to try and keep the mouse population under control. We didn't have much success.

Young Violet, our mail-order bride, was especially afraid of mice. She couldn't even bring herself to flip a dead one out of a trap, but waited 'til Benny came home to handle the corpse. She was a pretty brave girl usually. After all, she came all the way to Alaska to marry a man she'd never met and that takes courage. But mice apparently scared her more than men did.

Benny got her a twenty-two and taught her how to shoot it. They practiced on tin cans and bottles out at the dump until she felt comfortable handling it. She'd sit on a chair at the back of their cabin, point the gun at their wood pile and wait for a mouse to stick his nose out. The first couple of days she had no luck.

But on the third day, Miss Mousey crept out from between two logs and Violet let 'er have it. When she saw what she'd done, Violet cried. She was still crying when Benny came home from work. Sobbing into his sweaty shirt front, she vowed she'd never kill another thing as long as she lived.

As I said before, others in town didn't feel that way. They hunted and trapped for food, pelts and bounty money. So we often saw dead wolves, coyotes, beaver, lynx, rabbits, otters and even a mink or two.

Thank the good Lord, He didn't see fit to send us any snakes, lizards, scorpions or Gila monsters. Or a lot of other ornery critters I'd just as soon do without. Arizona and New Mexico can keep them.

For pure aggravation and misery, we had our mosquitoes, no-see-ums and white socks. I've heard there are thirty-five species of mosquitoes in Alaska, and I'll bet I've been acquainted personally with every single one.

So that's what I remember about Muckluck's animals. Just like people, some were tame and loveable and others were wild and ornery. You just had to know the difference and respect it.

~ 33 ~

One dark January, after the Christmas holidays had come and gone, some of our ladies decided we needed a club. When more interest was indicated, we got kinda excited about the idea.

We decided to name it the Muckluck Homemakers' Club and soon had a membership of somewhere around twenty women. Actually, it may not have been a club in the true sense of the word, as we didn't pay dues and had no officers.

Our club met at the schoolhouse the second Tuesday evening of the month. Val supplied a forty-cup coffee maker, and the coffee for it, and the rest of the ladies potlucked desserts, since we'd already eaten supper at home. We enjoyed getting together and decided a different member should supply the "program" each time.

The programs often were educational. One month Wilma taught us how to knit stocking caps and scarves. While some of us had five thumbs on each hand, others caught on right away. Of course, some of the gals already knew how to knit, so they lent a hand to the rest of us. Pretty soon everybody in Muckluck was sporting warm, colorful caps, mittens and scarves. Those woolens really brightened up the old place!

Minnie told us how to vary our sourdough recipe so it took on a different flavor whenever we needed a change. I personally enjoyed a little cinnamon in mine.

Esther Waldorf showed us how to make cute little moccasins to be worn as lapel pins. We cut them from felt and sewed tiny beads around the sole and ankle areas. They were so darn cute.

We began making them at our own homes and selling them at the store and Chez Buffet. When we saw how well they went over, we sent a batch of our best efforts to The Alaska Shop in Seward. We were thrilled when they sold out and ordered more.

Violet's special program involved making beautiful flowers from crepe paper. She'd learned how when she worked as a hired girl for a Mexican family back in Oregon. The flowers were every color you can imagine and sure gussied up our cabins.

Nell Dodson, our trained singer, tried her best to teach us to sing in harmony. It took a lot of patience and practice, but some of us finally got the hang of it. We were able to perform "Oh, Holy Night" at the next Christmas program. I still love to harmonize, though my voice is weak and cracked now. I sound like a rooster with a chest cold. Too bad. I was pretty tolerable back in those days.

Granny Annie made gorgeous quilts, so she taught us simple patterns. You'd be surprised how pretty a quilt you can make out of scraps of discarded clothes and fabrics. We traded off pieces so everyone had a variety of material to use. Sue Martin shared a lovely bed sheet. We all got a piece of that. Old, worn tablecloths supplied a goodly amount of useable pieces, too.

When my quilt was finished, it included pieces that came from a jacket Joe Sterns had worn out, Mr. Nielson's nightshirt, the little Moffit girl's outgrown Sunday school dress and Baby Carrington's summer blanket.

My, those quilts all were something. Not only were they simply beautiful, and warm, but each square held a memory. I keep mine stored in a cedar chest and bring it out ever so often when I need a pick-me-up.

Some months we didn't have a regular program, but one of the gals would read aloud an interesting article from the *Ladies Home Journal* or a story from *The Saturday Evening Post*. Then we'd discuss what she read.

Kinda like a scaled-down version of a book club. We couldn't have a real book club, because we didn't have enough books of one title to go around. That's okay, we were satisfied with our short stories and articles.

One time we got our heads together and sent a piece to the "Laughter is the Best Medicine" section of the *Reader's Digest*. I don't recall what the story was about, but I think it was something about the time some local boys nailed a privy door shut on Halloween while Burt Lawrence was inside. You could hear his howls all over town. We thought it was a scream.

The *Digest* paid good money if they published your little story, and we were hopeful. But we never heard back from them. We didn't hold it against them, though, and continued to read their magazine faithfully anyway. We learned a lot from the *Digest*.

The main goal of our little club was to try to be better homemakers. We tried to come up with ideas to make our humble homes more colorful, our work lighter, our food tastier and just to make life more enjoyable. Some years we even tackled community projects, like building swings and a teeter-totter for the school yard and painting St. Anastasia church. Those onion domes were the dickens — it's a wonder nobody got killed.

We decided to put on a little skit for the Muckluck Mid-Summer Madness festival one year. We practiced for weeks until we had our act down pat.

The seven performers in our ditty represented a grandmother, a father, a mother, a little girl and three passersby. Some of our ladies sewed the costumes, and they successfully decked out our little family as hillbillies.

Now keep in mind this was before "political correctness" came into fashion, so we didn't know any better. Grandma had her front teeth blacked out, sported powdered hair and wore a shawl.

Father tucked her hair into a cap, had a charcoal mustache and wore work overalls. She clenched a corn-cob pipe in her mouth.

Mother wore a tired work dress and men's shoes. She also had a "plug of tobaccy" in her cheek.

I, being short and round, was the little girl. My costume consisted of shorts, pigtails, painted freckles and bare feet.

We all carried various battered suitcases, paper bags and so forth onto our stage, where Dave Moffid had made a real nice railroad-crossing sign and some rails to serve as "props."

As our group approached the railroad tracks, we stopped short to read a sign: **Next Train To Nashville at 6:15**

We waited. Pretty soon a passerby came along.

"What time be it, kind sir?" asked Father.

The passerby looked at his pocket watch.

"Why, it's 4:42," he replied, and then went on his way.

We waited until the second passerby approached.

"What time is it, if you please?" asked Father.

"Oh, it's 5:20," came the reply.

The third person walked up to us.

"What time is it, please?" asked Father.

"It's 5:30," we were told. "Are you folks waiting for the 6:15 to Nashville?"

"No," we replied in unison. "We're just a-waitin' to cross the railroad tracks!"

I don't know, it seemed a lot funnier then. But maybe I'm not telling it right. It brought down the house at the Mid-Summer Madness festival.

The Homemakers Club waxed and waned for many years. Occasionally someone would get tired of the whole thing and drop out, but then there was always someone else who wanted to "belong."

Fresh blood always brought fresh ideas, and goodness knows we needed them. Women sometimes need to be reminded of their worth and that they're entitled to some fun, too.

I wrote a little poem for one of our get-togethers. Looking at it now, it's kinda corny. But some of the women memorized it, which made me real proud.

Celebrating Women

On calendars we mark a date
To set aside and celebrate.
There's New Year's Eve and Easter, too
July the Fourth, red, white and blue.

Thanksgiving brings good food and fun.
We cheer when Santa makes his run.
We celebrate at weddings, too
As bride and groom both vow "I do."

When babies come — we celebrate
And note their birthdays' special date.
Even Patrick (who's a Saint)
We celebrate without restraint.

We celebrate so often now
I wonder if we've missed somehow
To celebrate ourselves — yes, us!
We're special, too, let's make a fuss.

And tell the world we're here to say
That we deserve not just one day
But every day throughout the year.
We're women, so let's have a cheer!

We've got the strength, we've got the heart
To finish any task we start.
We've got the brains, and courage, too
To do the things we have to do.

So celebrate with all your might,
Be it morning, noon or night.
For we are women — sing our worth.
Proclaim our song throughout the earth!

~ 34 ~

Well, you're probably getting tired of all my stories by now. What's that? You're wondering how and why I left Muckluck, and why you can't find it on a map of Alaska? Well, that's a bitter-sweet story and not an easy one to tell. But since you've been so patient, I suppose you deserve to know.

I'd arrived at the point of being an "old maid."

Oh, I'd had my chances, so don't feel sorry for me. When we were teenagers, my good friend Leviticus suggested we get married, but I told him we were way too young to even think about it. I had worlds to conquer, and I didn't plan on getting tied down any time soon. He was mad for a while and wouldn't talk to me. But he got over it, and we went back to our former best-buddy relationship.

Olav also asked me to marry him after we'd been friends for years. I was truly dumbfounded, for although I admired and loved Olav as a pal, he just didn't "float my boat," as my grandkids say. When I refused as kindly as I could, he took it well. He just shrugged his shoulders and said, "Okay, just thought I'd ask. No hard feelings, Pal."

And that was the end of it. You'd think he would have put up more of a fight, but that was Olav. We remained good friends until he died, and I expect to see Olav again someday soon in a place even better than Muckluck.

Then there was a fella named Joe Smith who worked on the road crew one summer. He took a liking to me and asked me to be his wife. He wasn't my type at all, and I couldn't imagine going through life as Kate Smith!

What? You don't know about Kate Smith? Why, she was the most famous lady singer in America during the War. She had a voice that could rattle windows, and she sang "God Bless America" like she was giving a direct order to the Almighty. Anyway, I turned down Joe Smith, too. Kate Smith? I don't think so.

In my fortieth year, another stranger arrived in town. His name was Maximillion Charboneau, but insisted, "Just call me Max." He was about the handsomest fella I'd ever seen — tall, broad shouldered, slim-hipped, hair black as coal and blue eyes that twinkled when he laughed, which was often.

We learned he was French Canadian, but he'd left Canada many years before looking for his older brother. He'd searched all over Canada and many of the states, but a chance meeting with a former Alaskan suggested he should try looking there.

I was planting pansies with Father Sorinoff in front of the church when Max strolled up and introduced himself. We both were impressed by his striking looks and good manners. We gave our names, but before we could invite him in for coffee, he reached into his coat pocket and pulled out a photograph.

"Have you ever seen this man?" he asked.

And there he was — the stranger who'd died in my outhouse years before!

Father Sorinoff and I gasped, struck dumb. Max realized immediately that we recognized the man in the photo.

"You know him? Where is he?" Max asked.

We finally caught our breath. Father found his voice first.

"Yes, we recognize that man. I am so sorry to tell you that he passed away long ago," Father told him. "He didn't have any identification, so we claimed him as one of our own and buried him in our cemetery."

Max swallowed real hard, took two deep breaths and blinked his eyes a couple of times.

"Thank you," he said. "That's my brother. I'll be back to talk to you later," and he walked away real fast.

Father Sorinoff and I just stood there gaping as Max hurried off toward Moose Run. Then we wiped our hands and went inside the rectory for a cup of coffee and a long talk. Father said a real nice prayer for Max and his brother, and we both got kinda choked up.

Max came knocking at my door the next morning. He wanted to hear all I could tell him about his brother, Maurice.

I tried to pretty up the facts a bit, but I had to admit I'd found Maurice dead in my outhouse. I told him how Anchorage had sent authorities to investigate the death and then concluded he'd died of a heart attack. I told him how we had given his brother a proper, Christian burial and still were caring for his grave.

He asked to see the grave, so I took him out to the cemetery and pointed to the marker Dave Moffid had carved. Max read the inscription.

"Why, that's beautiful," he said. "Maurice would have liked that very much, and I appreciate what you folks did for him. I'm sorry he's gone, but now I know where he rests, and I guess my search is over."

He took my hands in his and looked deeply into my eyes.

"I think maybe I've found more than my brother here in Muckluck," he added.

I didn't know what he meant then, but before long he was seriously courting me. And I'll tell you, I didn't put up a fight. I fell so hard you could feel the earth shake.

We decided that since we weren't getting any younger, and would like to have a family, we'd better get started. So we went off to Anchorage, got a license and were married just a month after we met.

Because of our ages, we started on that family right away. I was expecting by our two-month anniversary, and I delivered twins nine months later. It was quite a scramble getting to the hospital in Anchorage in time.

I'd as soon have had them at home with Esther Waldorf assisting, but considering my age and that I was carrying twins, Max insisted on the hospital. So we had a little boy we named Maurice, but called Morry, and a girl we christened Carolyn.

I could write a book about raising those kids. Maybe some day I will — I'm that proud of them. But I've got to move along and finish telling you about Muckluck.

Max and I and the twins were still living in my old cabin. We'd put on a large addition to accommodate our growing family, and while it was still a little crowded, it was cozy and we liked it. Our lives were simple, peaceful and full of love.

On March 27, 1964, we thought Armageddon had arrived for sure. That was the day the Good Friday earthquake hit Alaska with a vengeance. It was a doozy, all right.

We'd just finished supper when it hit. Max was sitting by the stove studying an Atlas, marking his journeys when hunting for Maurice. The kids were doing their homework at the table, and I'd just started washing the dishes when the rumbling and shaking began. The whole cabin bucked like a bronco.

The doors to the cupboards flew open and dishes and canned goods crashed to the floor. A bag of Gold Medal flour exploded when it landed, spewing white dust over everything. I lost my footing and fell on my face.

The twins and Max staggered over to help me up, but we were all weaving like drunks, bumping into each other and the furniture. Then the cabin door crashed open.

I saw trees whipping back and forth, some dipping nearly to the ground. I heard dogs all over town howling and barking. And people screaming.

I've read it lasted less than five minutes, but it seemed like an hour. When the cabin stopped groaning and rolling like a ship at sea, we just sat there on the flour-dusted linoleum, looking at each other and wondering what to do first.

Max asked if we were all right. We checked each other out and found our bits and pieces were still intact. Max then pushed through the doorframe and practically fell outside. I followed him, but told the kids to stay indoors.

We saw huge cracks in the ground. Long, zigzag cracks, some nearly a foot wide. Moose Run had jumped its banks and flooded nearby land and homes. Trees were down, and many of the older cabins were, too. Muckluckers were running hither and thither, all yelling and calling out names of family and friends.

There were fires from wood stoves that had tipped over, and some homes were lost before we could douse the flames. We'd experienced lots of earthquakes — we were Alaskans. But nothing even came close to this catastrophe.

And it wasn't over. Several aftershocks followed. They weren't near as powerful as the big quake, but they were scary as all get-out just the same. You never knew when the next one might bring the end of the world. It was Good Friday, after all.

Eventually we calmed down. Everyone was present and accounted for — nobody was killed. Several people were banged up by falling debris, but Carol and a few helpers patched them up.

The worst injury was to Earl Raben. His brother, Mack, accidentally bumped him into a piece of their roof that had caved in. Earl broke his arm. He was sent to the hospital for a cast, but he was young and healed fast.

Muckluckers eyeballed the damage and found that nearly half the homes were beyond repair. The bucking, shifting ground had brought down the old cabins, crushing everything inside.

So families moved in with friends for a while, and then, all things considered, many moved away. Most of them moved Outside to areas not so prone to earthquakes. Some moved to the Midwest, where they dealt with tornadoes, or to the Southeast, where they had to put up with hurricanes. Others ended up in areas that had floods and mudslides. No matter where you go, nature has a way of showing you who's boss.

Those of us who stayed behind figured if it was your time to go, you were going to go. Ready or not. And we'd just as soon "go" in Muckluck. But it was awful hard seeing all those shattered homes and saying goodbye to so many good, dear friends.

The store was a complete loss, so Bing and Val moved on. Chef Buffet was so traumatized that he closed the restaurant and went back to France.

Some folks found it too difficult to live without having a store or restaurant close by, so they left, too. The loss of those businesses and long-time residents broke our hearts.

Those of us who stayed cleared away the rubble and tried to make the town livable again. Moose Run had changed its course and ran practically through the middle of town. Our cabin had become creek-front property.

The following year we sent the twins to Anchorage to attend high school. They boarded with Smokey and Bev Middleton, who moved there after the earthquake. Morry and Carolyn came home for holidays and summer vacation, but as they grew older, there was nothing for them to do.

It seems like in no time they were heading off to college at the University of Oregon. My, how those years flew by.

And then, when the kids were in their senior year of college, my world collapsed.

Max stepped out one evening to chop wood for the stove. He was gone a long time, so I went to see what he was up to.

I found him on the ground beside the chopping block, dead from a massive heart attack. He looked as beautiful in death as he did the first time I laid eyes on him. I loved him so much, I just wanted to lie down beside him and die, too.

But of course I didn't. I survived. As always.

We buried Max beside his brother, Maurice. I had Dave carve a double marker for the two of them.

Carol helped me through those dark days, but she kept talking about moving Outside. I knew I'd be losing her soon, too.

There were only a handful of people left in Muckluck a few years later. That's when the twins, who had each married and were starting their own families in Oregon, convinced me to move closer to them.

I hated like the dickens to leave Muckluck, Max and Alaska. But I was getting old and I didn't want to worry my kids.

~ 35 ~

In the fall of 1978, a bush pilot in a Piper Cub ran into mechanical problems. I read about it in *The Oregonian*. The plane fell from the sky like a rock, right in the middle of Muckluck.

The Cub burst into flames, which caught on the thirsty grass and tinder-dry trees. Soon what little remained of the town was ablaze. The few old-timers still hanging on fled for their lives.

The town was gone in an hour's time. Firefighters from Anchorage and Seward arrived too late to save a single building. That's why you won't find Muckluck on a map.

I never went back. Never wanted to. I'd rather remember it as it was. Now Muckluck is truly a place where "nothing ever happens."

Well, that was quite a gabfest, wasn't it? I just about talked your ears off, you poor thing. I hope you enjoyed my stories half as much as I enjoyed telling them.

I'm tired now. It's time for a nap. Just tuck that afghan up under my chin, and close the door when you leave. There, that's a good child....

Homecoming

Come, pause with me while I spin tales
Of long ago and far away,
Where snow-clad mountains sweep the sky
And dip their toes into the bay.
A place where eagles scream and soar,
Where still the lynx and coyotes roam
Who share the space and wilderness
With moose and bear, who feel at home
Among the spruce and willow trees;
Where ermine slinks and horned owls
Glide through the dark and silent night.
The grey wolf lifts his head and howls.

I'll sing of raging rivers wild
With waters, nectar sweet and cold
That tumble, icy, glacier fed
And hide elusive hordes of gold.
Aurora borealis whips
Across the black expanse of sky.
She moans unearthly, mystic tones:
The song which ghosts or angels cry.
Frost-coated limbs of frigid trees
Snap and crackle as they taste
The kiss of winter on their boughs,
Indulge the season's chill embrace.

Life's journey led me far away
From scenes of childhood, now so dear
That fill my dreams and tell the tales
That fall so gently on my ear.
Yet some day when I'm laid to rest
Back in my homeland vast and wild
They'll place a stone upon my breast:
"Here lies a proud Alaskan child."

www.ingramcontent.com/pod-product-compliance
Lightning Source LLC
Chambersburg PA
CBHW071007280626
47160CB00015B/1672